REALMGOLDS

REALMGOLDS

The Gryphon Clerks (Book 1)
by Mike Reeves-McMillan

DIGITAL SCIENCE FICTION

DIGITAL FICTION
PUBLISHING CORP

Copyright © 2017 Mike Reeves-McMillan
Edition copyright © 2017 Digital Fiction Publishing Corp.
All rights reserved. 2nd Edition (US Eng)
ISBN-13 (paperback): 978-1-927598-58-0
ISBN-13 (e-book): 978-1-927598-57-3
Cover art by Chris Howard (saltwaterwitch.com)

For Erin, my own heroic civil servant.

Chapter 1: A Scintillating Evening of Valuable Progress

The young man seated at the heavy old desk sighed and let a sheaf of papers drop to the desk's cluttered surface. It was a report on the Human Purity movement and its leader, Admirable Silverstones, the Countygold of Upper Hills. Its contents gathered his forehead into a frown.

The light was fading, and the stone-floored room, always chilly, edged toward cold. He reached over and touched the sigil on the base of the brass desk lamp, which released its cool illumination into the room as he muttered the Dwarvish word for light. Then he spoke the spell which adjusted the tall black iron warming columns set on either side of his chair. Like most of the other furniture in the room, they were old. He smelled the scent of toasting linen from his shirtsleeve, and adjusted them back down again. His feet resumed freezing, despite two pairs of socks.

Concentrating on the devices, he barely heard a tentative tap at the door.

"Yes, Reliable?" he called out.

His secretary, Reliable Chandler, poked his rabbitlike face around the door.

"Your pardon, Realmgold," he said, addressing his master by his title. "Did you intend to join your Provincegolds in their quarterly meeting tonight?"

"Have I been invited this time?"

The secretary dropped his eyes, and colored. "Ah, not as such, Realmgold. But as it is being held here in Lakeside Koslin this quarter…"

"Quite. When is it?"

"According to the minutes of the last meeting," said the secretary, advancing into the room with a piece of paper, "at the twelfth deep bell." He placed the paper on the desk, his finger indicating the information at the bottom.

The young Realmgold, whose given name was Determined, narrowed his eyes when he noticed that the last, and uncompleted, item on the previous agenda was the Human Purity movement. He glanced at the elaborate dwarfmade clock in the corner. "That gives me time to read these minutes, then." He flipped the paper over to begin on the first side.

The secretary coughed. "And might I suggest a fresh shirt, Realmgold?"

Determined glanced down at his ruffled cuffs, marked with ink-splatters and dust. "You may. Have one brought down. And my green coat. If it's this cold inside, I hate to think what it's like in the street."

The way out led through the Realmgolds' Gallery, and Determined frowned up at the larger-than-life-size portraits of his predecessors. Studying history at the College of Ancient

Turfrae, he'd experienced an odd double awareness of them as both historical figures and his own ancestors. He could trace every mistake they'd made, every unwise compromise or concession, and the reasons, good and bad. He gave a special glare to his great-great-grandmother, inappropriately named Prudence, who had put the Provincegolds in charge of collecting (and reporting) the realmtax in their provinces and accelerated the loss of power and influence of the office of Realmgold.

"And so here I am today," he muttered to himself.

"Beg pardon, Realmgold?" said Reliable.

"Nothing," said Determined.

The Provincegold Lake had a town house almost opposite the Realmgold's palace. As Determined strode across the street, his footfalls rang off the cobbles, the echoes muted by the decorative vines growing up the walls of both buildings. With Reliable trailing a step behind and to the right, he marched up the marble steps to Lake's door.

A retainer in the Provincegold's livery stepped forward as if to stop him, but Determined simply met his gaze with raised eyebrows and kept on walking. The man stepped back, raising his hands in an "I'm not getting involved" gesture.

A grey-haired man in a long blue coat, attended by a young woman in a similar coat tailored for her much slimmer figure, were making their way up the internal staircase. The woman heard Determined's footsteps, echoed by the lighter and more tentative steps of his secretary, and glanced behind her. He recognized Courtesy Hollowtrees of Westcoast, accompanying her father, the Provincegold Westcoast. She turned back around without giving him so much as a nod.

His few conversations with Courtesy had only demonstrated that they had nothing in common, but that stung nevertheless.

He was right behind them when they entered the tea room at the top of the stairs, and gave his best aristocratic glare to the retainer on the door, who, like his colleague downstairs, didn't quite dare to stop the Realmgold.

There were, of course, only enough chairs for the Provincegolds and their invited guests, mostly heirs, advisors or secretaries. The hostess, Felicity Lake, took in the Realmgold's presence without visible emotion and signaled the retainer to fetch two more seats.

When tea had been served and sipped and little spiced cakes had been sampled, the Provincegold Lake set down her delicate teacup and leaned back as a sign that business could now be discussed. The others ceased their conversations — none of which were with Determined — and turned their heads toward her.

"At our last meeting, we were speaking," she said in her languid style, "of Human Purity."

"And I was saying," said gruff Westcoast, "that you want to keep an eye on your lad there." The county of Upper Hills, Silverstones' demesne, lay within the Province of Lake.

"You oppose his philosophy?" said Tenacious Northriver, throwing his head back and staring at the older man with his hands on his hips. His nostrils flared.

"Not at all," said Westcoast. "I disapprove, however, of letting one's Countygolds build up too much of a following."

This brought wise nods from around the room.

"Who says I'm not controlling him from behind the scenes?" said Lake.

"Are you?" asked Northriver, forehead wrinkled. Northriver tended to need things explained.

Lake didn't answer, just gave him a bland look.

"It's not just your province that's affected, though," said Thousand Hills, a tremulous, querulous older woman. "The dwarves in my province have come to me asking what I'm doing about protecting them and their assets. There's a lot of mining in Thousand Hills, you know."

Everyone was well aware of the mining in Thousand Hills.

"What did you tell them?" asked Westcoast.

"I said I'd study the matter, of course," she said. There were more nods. This was a reliable stall.

"I don't see the problem," said Northriver. "They're not doing anything wrong. They're allowed their opinions under the Code of Willing."

"They're allowed their own religious and philosophical opinions," Determined said. "Political opinions are another matter." He had tried to hold himself back from speaking, but he couldn't let that one go. He had studied the ancient Code of Willing, the foundation of all human law, intensively while at the College of Ancient Turfrae.

Nobody took up his point.

"Their philosophy gives the disaffected and the underemployed among the Copper class something to do with their excess energy," said Southcliffs, a middle-aged man with a weatherbeaten face. "I don't see the harm."

"Easy for you to say," quavered Thousand Hills. "Plenty to do already in your province."

"No fault of mine that your hills don't grow much grain," snapped Southcliffs. "Most of the troublemakers I do have come down over the border looking for work I don't have."

The discussion dissolved into a rehearsal of grievances going back three generations between the two neighboring provinces, and it took some time for Lake to bring it back on track.

"We were discussing," she said, "Human Purity." By her standards, she spoke emphatically. "And Consolation, I get plenty of your people too, by the way. Hard workers, as a general thing." Thousand Hills preened at the small, if backhanded, compliment, and shot a glare at Southcliffs, but stopped complaining.

"Perhaps," said Beauty Six Gorges, the only provincegold who had not so far spoken, "we should talk about why there are so many disaffected people in the first place."

"It's Koskant's fault," said Southcliffs immediately. "If they didn't have the gulf trade locked up..."

"Failing crops..." put in Thousand Hills.

"Greedy Nine-cursed dwarves," said Northriver. "And those centaurs across my river..."

One by one, each provincegold managed to find a reason why it wasn't his or her fault that the people weren't prosperous. Six Gorges listened patiently, swiveling her head from one speaker to the next. As her eyes passed across Determined's, she twitched one eyelid very slightly at exactly the moment that their gazes met, and despite his distress at the way the meeting was going, he had to purse his lips to keep from smiling.

When the litany of complaint subsided, Six Gorges said, "I think it's wonderful that you've all done so much to overcome the problems your people face, so that only factors beyond your control are left. Truly, wonderful. So I suppose the only question left to ask is, do we take a joint position on this Human Purity movement, or do we... study the matter further and deal with it individually?"

She habitually kept her face still, presumably to keep from cracking her makeup, and her voice was carefully modulated, so most of the provincegolds missed the sarcasm, Determined thought. Northriver certainly would have, but Northriver would miss being hit with a sack of rocks. Lake, he thought, would have got it, but her expression didn't change either as she resumed control of the meeting.

"Thank you, Beauty, that is exactly the question before us. Let us have the sense of the meeting now, and if we decide for a joint response we can talk about what that will be afterwards. In order of seniority, then. Consolation?"

"Individually," said Thousand Hills. "We all have very different problems in our provinces, after all."

Lake turned to Westcoast, the next oldest, with a questioning look. He also voted for an individual response.

So did Southcliffs. "Let's see," Lake said, "who's next?" She turned to Six Gorges. "Beauty?"

Claws of the cat, thought Determined. The two women were about the same age, but Lake looked several years older.

"Oh, is it me?" said Six Gorges. "I forget you're a little younger, Felicity. For what it's worth, I think we should have a joint response, but I fear I'm already outvoted."

Lake merely nodded, and voted individual. Predictably, so did Northriver, the youngest of the six.

"That's settled, then," said Lake. "We each make our own response, though we keep the option open to discuss a joint position at our next meeting. Which is in your province, I believe, Tenacious."

7

Northriver nodded, drawing himself up self-importantly. "Yes, I look forward to seeing you there in a quarter of a year," he said.

"Very good," said Lake. "As usual, all of you are invited to dine. Oh, Determined, I'm sorry, dear, I didn't expect you, so I haven't catered accordingly."

This was a flimsy and transparent excuse to exclude him from the meal, where, no doubt, the real business of the evening would be transacted. Years of training not to make a scene overruled the familiar angry helplessness stinging behind his eyes.

"No apology necessary, Lake," he said, using her name of affiliation rather than her personal name to emphasize the distance between them, but not referencing her title since she hadn't used his. He bowed the merest inch. "I am well suited across the street. Come, Reliable."

She bowed back, just detectably lower, and removed her attention from him entirely. Nobody else paid him any either, except Six Gorges, who also bowed to him as he passed. He leaned close, covered by the hubbub of conversation, and whispered, "I'd like to talk."

"Sixth bell," she whispered back, and he nodded and left the room.

"Well," Determined remarked to Reliable, as they crossed the darkened street, "that was a scintillating evening filled with valuable progress."

The little secretary didn't comment.

Chapter 2: Beauty

Halfway between dawn and noon the following day, just as the sixth deep bell rang out from the High Temple's astronomy tower, a footman showed Beauty into Determined's office. She shed the plain hooded cloak she wore over her stylish clothes and handed it off to the footman to hang for her.

She was not, Determined had always thought, actually beautiful, if you looked at her closely, but she presented herself so well that most people probably thought of her as matching her name.

It wasn't required by protocol, but Determined rose and came out from behind his desk to lay his forearm along hers in the traditional greeting of High Golds. He gestured the Provincegold to a seat in front of his desk and returned to sit behind it.

"Beauty, it's a pleasure to see you, as always," he said, as the door opened and admitted Reliable.

She gave a graceful nod. The secretary seated himself discreetly on a small chair to the side of the office, with his notepad and pencil ready.

Beauty's eyes roamed over the walls for a few moments. "The books are new, aren't they?" she said.

"Most of the bookshelves, too," said Determined. "My uncle was..." He paused, seeking a tactful way to describe the previous Realmgold.

"More interested in horses," Beauty supplied.

"And wine," Determined muttered.

"An unfortunate combination, as it turned out," she said. "For him, at least."

For me as well, he thought, but didn't say.

"I gained the impression, Beauty," Determined said, turning to business, "that we might have matters to discuss."

"Well, Determined," she said, taking his cue and using his given name, "this is my situation. I have the only province that has no external borders, not to mention that it's full of rocks and if you smoothed out the cliffs it would be twice the size. I am dependent, therefore, on the goodwill of my neighbors, but I am also affected by their troubles and their bad decisions. If Northriver offends the centaurs, it becomes harder for me to sell them leather. If Southcliffs mistreats his port workers and they riot, it becomes harder for me to ship wine to Koskant. And if there's general civil unrest and the gnomes and dwarves keep a low profile, it costs me extra to buy tools. None of those problems are insuperable. I don't fling up my hands and blame everyone else, like some provincegolds I could mention. But it makes it harder. Accordingly, I'm in favor of national unity, which means I'm inevitably inclined towards a strong realmgold."

"Unfortunately you and I appear to be the only ones," said Determined ruefully. "Convincing the rest of that is like selling gritty melons."

"It is. So we need to work with the situation we have, and try to get it closer to the one we want. I can't fix everyone else's province, but I'm doing what I can with mine."

"You're doing very well," he said. "The new mage school, the schools in general…"

"I have limited funds," she said. "I asked myself, how can I create the most prosperity in the shortest time with the funds I have? And then I looked at what young Victory is doing down in Koskant, and the answer was obvious. Educate the people, do it well, and then everything else becomes easier."

"But I have to assume," he said, "that you are losing graduates to other provinces?"

"I do my best to create appropriate challenges for my graduates to meet," she said. "But yes, there's a certain amount of outflow. They do tend to send back money, though, so it's not entirely a bad thing."

"If I announced a realmwide initiative to improve education…"

"You'd face all kinds of opposition, but yes, it's a good idea. Perhaps you could set aside, say, an eighth of the realmtax?"

"How about a sixteenth?" he countered. "Of the realmtax I actually get, that is. If you get stopped by a bandit, I'm sorry, by a rural localgold in one of the more remote areas of the Realm of Denning, he'll claim to be collecting taxes on my behalf, but if you press him, he'll admit that he spares me the administrative overhead of actually sending them in. After all, he claims, the money would only come back out again, or else be wasted by definition."

"So generous," she smiled.

"Indeed. Yet, as you say, education is the best place to start spending the money we do have, and it should start to combat this Human Purity nonsense as well, since that's based on pure ignorance and stupidity."

"I'm having difficulty working out whether you're in favor of Human Purity or not," the Provincegold said with a straight face.

"Yes, well. Dwarves may be moneygrubbing little sods, but at least you always know where you stand. They negotiate hard, but fairly. And the centaurs are decent people, in my experience. I'd take most of the ones I've met ahead of a good many humans, the other provincegolds not excepted. Unfortunately when the Countygold of Upper Hills tells the common people that all their problems are someone else's fault, he gets a ready hearing. And when he suggests beating up the beasthead people and the gnomes and the dwarves and the centaurs and anyone else who doesn't look, talk and think, or rather refuse to think, exactly like they do, and then taking their lunches...."

"Quite," she said, with a slight smile. "But you'll need to be careful about opposing Human Purity. Admirable may be a ranting little jackass," she deliberately echoed his description of the dwarves, "but he's a demagogue of some skill, and he already has the sympathy of a lot of the High Golds as well as the Copper peasantry."

"What about the Silvers?" he said.

"Most of the merchants and craftspeople deal with dwarves personally and know he's talking nonsense," she said. "But they're not as big a group as the Coppers, or as powerful as the Golds."

They talked strategy and options for well over an hour,

with Reliable scribbling notes in the corner.

"All right," said Determined at last. "So our agreement is this. I will promote educational programs wherever and whenever I can, and that includes providing more funding for the programs you already have, and hiring some of your graduates to teach elsewhere, with a bounty back to your province. You will provide me as much political support as you can, consistent with not breaking openly with the other provincegolds, and I will press for the abolition of internal tariffs for trade between provinces. I'd also like to continue to share ideas about how to oppose Human Purity and Silverstones' so-called Realm Benefit Party."

"Thank you, Determined," she said. "It's been a pleasure."

"For me also," he said, rising and coming to touch forearms again. "My greetings to your oathmate and sons, by the way."

"Thank you, I'll pass those on."

Reliable summoned the footman, who helped Beauty back into her cloak. When she had gone, Determined sank down behind his desk again with a pleased sigh.

"I think we may finally be making progress," he said to Reliable. "It feels good to *do* something."

Chapter 3: A Farviewer for Determined

Determined looked up when the courier horn sounded. He had always loved the huge white flying horses that the skycouriers rode, and stood up from his desk to stretch, walk over to the window, and watch the landing. He recognized Thorn White, who was based at Gulfport in Koskant, as she came in downwind to the courtyard set aside for the couriers. Her skyhorse, The Zephyr, had a distinctive swooping glide which ended in a flare of his enormous white wings and a perfect galloping touchdown.

Determined wasn't expecting anything from Koskant, his realm's southern neighbor — particularly anything as large as the parcel strapped to Thorn's back. He returned to his desk and fidgeted with papers as he waited for the courier to make her way up to his office.

Thorn wore the usual white flying suit and helmet with goggles, and a vest covered with white feathers from her skyhorse's wings. Her white leather riding boots clicked crisply on the stone floor between the slightly worn woven rugs. She was accompanied by one of the palace footmen, who wrestled the bulky flat package Determined had glimpsed from his window.

"Package direct to the Realmgold's hand." She gestured to the footman to lean it against a chair, which he did, bowing carefully before stretching his aching back. Determined made a gesture of dismissal, and the man faded out of the room.

"From?" asked Determined.

"Koskant, is all I know, Realmgold. But I was given it by a gnome who works for the Koskant Realmgold's clever man."

"Containing?"

The courier blinked. "Not my job to know, Realmgold. I just deliver them. But there's this note."

"Hmm," said Determined, taking the sealed note, which was blank on the outside. He ripped it open and scanned it. It told him to be alone when he opened the package.

"All right," he said, "you may go."

She bowed and followed the footman through the door, which Reliable closed behind them.

Determined took out a small dagger and began to tear open the parcel.

It contained a large piece of tinted glass in a simple frame, about the size of a head-and-shoulders portrait, with a crystal set into the frame at the top. There was also another note.

"My dear northern neighbor," the note read. "I suggest you call for an artist's easel to support this device. To activate it, touch the crystal and say 'start' clearly in Dwarvish. Once you have done so, you will learn something to your advantage, I hope. Please be alone when you activate the device."

Like the note directing him to open the package alone, it

was signed "Victory Highcliffs" and marked with a gryphon seal. Not, he noted, with the ship in full sail which was the Koskant seal, and Victory didn't style herself "Realmgold of Koskant". This made it a personal note, not an official exchange between monarchs.

Intrigued, he stuck his head into the outer office and had his secretary arrange for an artist's easel to be brought up.

A footman had to be sent to a shop outside the palace, and it was a good 45 minutes later that Determined dismissed the footman, lifted the device onto the easel himself from its partial concealment behind his desk, stripped off the rewrapped packaging and, trembling slightly with pent-up anticipation, worked the activation spell.

He knew that what it did wouldn't include exploding. A magical device could not be deliberately made to do so, since the Protocols of Hesh bound mages not to cause direct harm to others with magic, and nobody would dare to abuse the legendary neutrality of the skycouriers that way in any case. And Victory was an ally, bound by magical treaty not to send arms across the border. Regardless, he was almost as nervous as if he expected it to assassinate him.

It did not. Instead, it crackled with a sound like heavy rain and an appearance like heavy snow, and then cleared to show a woman in her mid-thirties, dressed in a simple, but well-cut white shirt and trousers, and seated in what appeared to be a comfortable Gold's tea-room, furnished with exquisite taste. The plush lemon-yellow sofa where she sat was the main note of color in the room, which also held, as far as he could see from his angle, one plain table with an elegant tea-set in glowing white porcelain, one shelf on which sat an abstract, polished wooden sculpture of a flowing, flamelike shape around a central void, and one pure black curtain.

He had met Victory after his accession as Realmgold, five years before, when he visited her capital to renew the ancient magical treaty between their realms. She looked the same age now as she had then, though her dark hair was now worn in a different style, braided and coiled on top of her head. He had been deeply impressed, at the time, with the deference everyone showed to her — a relatively young Realmgold, albeit older than him — and the confident way in which she ran her realm. She had given him a book, he recalled, and he wondered where he'd put it.

"Ah, Determined," she said, setting aside some papers. "So pleased to see you again."

"You can see me?" he asked.

"Yes. Rather wonderful, isn't it? My clever man just invented these. We are all those hundreds of thousands of dwarfpaces apart, and yet we can converse. Discreetly," she added.

"Discreetly. Yes. Victory," he said, taking her cue and calling her by her given name, "what is all this about?"

"Sometimes," she said, "one needs to talk to people. Just as people. Even if those people are also, let us say, important people. To discuss, calmly and directly, as neighbors, developments that affect us both."

"Do your advisors know you're talking to me?" he asked, suspecting the answer.

"No. Do yours?"

"No, I followed your instructions. We're alone. That is to say, I'm alone."

"As am I. So, as I was saying, there are some developments that affect us both, and by the time they are filtered through layers of officials, however well-meaning, there might well be distortion. I felt that, in such an important matter, this was unacceptable."

"What matter is that?"

"What is your view on Human Purity?"

"I would suppress it if only I could," he answered, with an honesty that surprised him.

"I had hoped that you would say that," she said.

"You have to understand," he said, "I don't have the control of public opinion you do. You make no secret of your contempt for Human Purity, I know, but it isn't as strong there in the south as it is here. The young Golds and a lot of the Coppers... I have to be careful what I say."

"Oh, I don't have control of public opinion," said Victory with an amused smile. "There's a free press in Koskant. What I do have is influence."

"I'm sure," he said, skeptically.

"It is only the truth," she said. "If some of the newspapers print what I want them to print it is not because I make them, but because I make it easier for them than printing the opposite. Newswriters are lazy, and if you give them a true story with a judicious touch of balance so that it is not completely one-sided, fifteen out of sixteen of them will change three commas and an adjective, put their name on it and print it. The sixteenth will investigate, find that it is essentially correct, rewrite it with a couple of additional facts, and print it."

"I wish I knew how to do that," he said. "I don't suppose you'd teach me?"

She looked at him levelly across the magical connection.

"My dear neighbor," she said, "that is exactly what I

intend to do."

The following day, Determined had his chief intelligencer send in an expert on Koskant.

"Tell me about Victory," he said.

The man, a nondescript fellow like most of the intelligencers, smiled. "One of the youngest realmgolds to be elected in Koskant," he said. "Formerly the Provincegold of Western, succeeding her grandfather. Generally considered one of the most intelligent, competent and all-around formidable rulers alive today. She has the loyalty and admiration of her people, although the more conservative Golds and some very wealthy Silvers oppose her."

"Have you ever met her?" asked the Realmgold.

"In person? No," said the intelligencer. "I've only seen her from a distance." He smiled again, wistfully, Determined thought.

"I get the impression you admire her."

"Realmgold, everyone admires her, or at least respects her. Even her chief opponent, the Provincegold of Gulfhead, calls her 'that magnificent....'" The intelligencer stopped, flushed a little, and concluded, "uh, he calls her an opprobrious name that I won't repeat, Realmgold, but he does say 'magnificent'."

"I have visited the stables, you know," said Determined mildly. "I've heard most of the words."

"Nevertheless, Realmgold," said the man. Determined had never seen an intelligencer embarrassed before, and it seemed to be because he couldn't bring himself to speak ill of the ruler of the country he spied on.

"Is she beautiful?" asked the Realmgold. He had his own

opinion, but wanted to hear another. The man considered his answer for several seconds.

"No," he said finally. "She is... Elegant. Striking. She has a strong face, but I don't think she could be called beautiful. And she always dresses in simple clothing, what they call in Koskant now a Victory suit, a plain but well-made shirt and trousers. It's a statement, I think, that she's not like her predecessor, old Glorious, who frankly dressed like a parrot. Always pure white, her suit is, and nobody else dares wear one in white, although practically all of her Gryphon Clerks wear them."

"Ah, yes, the Gryphon Clerks. What about them?"

"They're more than just civil servants, Realmgold. Far more. Their college provides more than vocational training, it gives very effective indoctrination into Victory's view of the world and her ideals for society. They emerge from it well-trained and devotedly loyal to her. Because it's such good training, the Silver class often send their brightest sons and daughters there to get a grounding that will help them when they take over the business, but most of them stay beyond the five years that is required after their training, and very few take the buyout option that lets them leave sooner."

"Interesting. What are her weaknesses?"

"She isn't a planner," said the intelligencer without hesitation. Determined imagined that considering the weaknesses of other rulers was a key part of intelligencing, even if the ruler concerned was bound by magical treaty not to send force of arms into Denning. "Her motto is that plans meet chaos as soon as they are implemented, but chaos favors the prepared."

"That sounds familiar."

"The Red General, Realmgold. Her favorite writer."

"Ah, yes, I remember now, that was the book she gave me. I think I still have it somewhere." He gestured to the bookcases lining his study walls.

"If you want to understand Victory, Realmgold, I would hunt it out and read it. As I was saying, she doesn't plan elaborately, she builds up as many different resources as she can and then acts spontaneously, in the confidence that she can deal with whatever comes up. She's usually right, to give her her due, though it's a somewhat wasteful approach. And she gives her trusted people what some consider excessive latitude. She makes sure that they understand her goals and philosophy, that they're competent and intelligent, and then she turns them loose to improvise. Again, I have to say it often works. She has some truly remarkable people serving her."

"How does that come to be, do you think? Are they drawn to her from round the world?"

"No, they're almost all Koskanders. But she does draw the best people of her realm to work for her rather than, as they might otherwise do, work for themselves or in the service of some other person or group. She offers them better challenges and more freedom, you see. Not necessarily more money — these are the kind of people for whom money is often not that important as long as they have enough for daily needs. She offers them the chance to participate in something they believe in. And, of course, Koskant is a wealthy trading nation, and there has been a tradition for generations of establishing schools, so the Silver population is well-educated."

"I understand she's begun encouraging the education of

Coppers, as well," said Determined.

"Yes, that's one of her more controversial policies. The conservative Golds and Silvers are not entirely happy with the thought of Coppers getting ideas above their station."

"What's her reason for doing it, do you know?"

"According to a speech she made at the opening of one of the schools, she thinks it's a waste of potential for Coppers to be restricted to manual labour when there are potentially great minds among them. And she believes — she says — that the strength and prosperity of a realm is built upon the strength and prosperity of the greatest number of people, regardless of their background. Wealth doesn't move from the top down, but from the bottom up."

"Interesting theory. Is it working?"

"Well, Koskant was already prosperous under the previous Realmgold, but under Victory its wealth has more than doubled in twelve years."

"So you would advise me to follow a similar approach if the opportunity presented itself?"

The man was disconcerted. "Uh, Realmgold, I am an intelligencer, not an adviser. I wouldn't presume to..."

"Tell me honestly. Do you think Denning would be a better place if it were more like Koskant? And do you think that I would be a better ruler if I were more like Victory?"

Determined caught the intelligencer's startled eyes and held them for two heartbeats before the man looked down and muttered, "Yes, Realmgold."

"Thank you," said Determined. "You've been most informative. You may go."

The man bowed and left.

Chapter 4: News and Events

That evening, Determined had the magic mirror moved to his quarters. He had another conversation with Victory scheduled, and wanted to conduct it in a less formal setting — though his quarters, which he hadn't got around to redecorating out of his uncle's style, were formal enough, he supposed.

Just short of the appointed time, he activated the mirror and was pleased to find Victory just activating her end.

"Good evening," he said.

"Good evening. Ah, your quarters?"

"Yes. I wanted to chat more comfortably."

"Good." She sat down on the pale yellow sofa. "I must admit, I am looking forward to knowing you better, Determined. I have heard good reports of you," she said, pouring herself a cup of tea.

"You have?" he said, with more eagerness than he intended.

"Yes, you have been described to me as probably the most intelligent person ever to rule Denning."

"Thank you, but I assure you, that's an easy distinction to

have achieved," he said wryly. "Intelligence hasn't traditionally been a factor in selecting Realmgolds here."

"So I understand. How is it that you got through?"

"Compromise candidate," he said, not meeting her eyes. "My cousins can't agree on much, except that most of them can't stand each other. My uncle hadn't nominated an heir, and when he died unexpectedly and the family had to elect a new head, I was the only eligible person whom nobody particularly disliked."

"Not the worst reason for succession I ever heard. What would you have done, had you not become Realmgold?"

"I was at the College of Ancient Turfrae. I was sent there to study law, government and mindmagic, like every other Gold, but I ended up doing graduate work in history. I wanted to teach."

Victory gave him an assessing look.

"Why history?"

"I wanted to understand how things happen."

"And what would that give you?"

He thought about that for an uncomfortably large number of heartbeats. Finally, he said quietly, "If I understand things, I feel like I'm in control. And I don't feel like that very often in my life. Even now, I get as much information about the realm as I can, because if I can't change what happens, at least I can know what happens."

Victory nodded. "You wanted to study history," she said, "and now you must make it, one way or another. Do you know how the skycouriers capture their horses?"

"I always assumed they bred them," he said, surprised at the change of topic.

"No, all the courier horses are young stallions, driven out

of the herds by their fathers. A young woman from the White clan will study specific kinds of mindmagic for many years, and when she is ready she finds such a stallion's feeding grounds. Often, she must climb into the mountains and find a meadow surrounded by peaks, where the horse flies down to feed. When she locates such a place, she sets out apples overnight."

"Apples?"

"Yes, skyhorses are very fond of apples, I'm told. Also, they are more curious and intelligent than an ordinary wingless horse. After a few nights, she starts putting the apples in the centre of a white cloth that smells of her, and she gradually bundles the cloth up so that it looks more and more like a human figure. Then, one night, she goes out there herself, lies down in the meadow and puts apples on her stomach, on her chest, and in her mouth."

"That's fascinating, but…"

"When the skyhorse comes to look for his apples, the young woman is in a form of preparatory trance, with her eyes closed," Victory continued. "When she feels the horse bite into the apple that she holds in her mouth, she opens her eyes and holds his gaze, and they bond in that moment. She continues to visit the meadow and feed him apples, and gradually she teaches him to bear her as a rider. They learn together, she to guide, he to be guided and influenced. But he is still a wild creature at heart, and the bond between them is not one of control. It's one of trust and understanding. Do you see?"

"I do. That… helps. Thank you. But how do I ride the Denning skyhorse? What are my apples?"

"Determined, I am going to speak frankly, and I ask you

not to take offense."

"Of course, Victory. Say what you wish. It's unlikely to be worse than my private thoughts."

"It's well known that your effective rule, and that of the Realmgolds of Denning for generations, doesn't extend all that far from Lakeside Koslin."

"True," sighed Determined. "The Provincegolds are fiercely independent and spend their time scheming against me, each other, and their Countygolds. The Localgolds are, for the most part, little more than brigands. And the Realm as a whole, if there is such an entity, is mired in poverty and conflict. The Realmgolds for generations have been..." He pinched the air with his right hand in a word-seeking gesture. "Inadequate."

"Would you like to change that?"

"Of course I would. I've been trying to work out how for five years now. But where do I start?"

"Well, building your popularity with the common people is never a bad place to begin, for all sorts of reasons. There are more of them, for one thing."

"And how do I do that? I'm a bookish, administrative Realmgold who rarely comes out of his office. Most of my people don't even know what I look like."

"How are you at public speaking?"

"I do it as briefly and as infrequently as possible."

"Are you willing to change that? Because if you don't change anything, you won't change anything."

He paused for a long breath before saying, "All right. I'm willing. But you'll have to teach me how."

"How much sleep do you need?"

"About a quarter of a day, if I'm disciplined."

"You know Cheerful of Narrowneck's *The Methods of Sleep*?"

"Yes, that's what got me down to a quarter of a day."

"Good. Re-read it, and apply *everything*. You'll need it. Do you follow a dietary plan?"

"Loosely. The Order of Westfields."

"Follow it closely. And do you know the Seventeen Movements of Strength and Balance?"

"My tutor taught them to me when I was a boy, but I haven't kept them up."

"Start them again. Find a teacher, there must be one in your capital. And one more thing."

"What's that?"

Victory took a deep breath. "Tomorrow, I will send you a small book. It is a series of preliminary exercises for a forgotten form of mindmagic. Practice them along with the rest."

"Did I pass a test?"

"You did. You understood the horse analogy, and you asked how you could learn to ride."

He regarded her image in the magic mirror. "Why are you doing this, Victory?" he asked.

"Apart from the fact that I would much rather deal with you than that ranting lunatic Silverstones? Because the ancient treaty between our realms currently protects Denning better than it does Koskant," she said. "My predecessor but three, Realmgold Tenacious, centralized anyone who had anything to do with public order, public safety or defense of the realm into the same military structure. Court and prison officers, Golds' bodyguards, civil emergency personnel, City Guards, coastal defense, intelligencers, everyone from my most senior generals to an eighteen-year-old village warden who protects six cottages and a hay-barn, are all under my command, and none of them can cross the Koslin River under arms because of that treaty.

"In Denning, though, you as Realmgold control a small minority of the armed forces. A localgold can send his troops across the river, and there's nothing you can do about it, in practice, though in theory it's an act of treason. It will be better for my realm if we change that."

He nodded. "That makes sense. Thank you, Victory. I count myself lucky that your interests lie in strengthening my position, rather than the reverse."

The leading newspaper in Denning was the *Eye of Lakeside*. On that same first day of Late Harvest, it ran a new column: The Realmgold Thinks.

Determined had decided to start his approach to doing more public speaking slowly, by doing more public writing. His first attempt was inoffensive, unspecific, and brief:

In this time of national controversy and division, it is fitting to consider the history and shared identity which we hold together as Denningers. Ever since Denning was a realm within the Elven Empire, we have considered ourselves one people. Whatever our differences may be among ourselves, let us never forget our essential unity.

We face many challenges at the moment, not least of them our constant struggle to improve the prosperity of our realm and its population — all of its population. It is my firm belief that by improving the lot of our Coppers, our Silvers will also prosper, and when the Silvers prosper the Golds are at peace.

I am myself an educated man, and know the value of education. By improving education among the Copper class, I believe we will see realmwide improvements in our standard of living and will be able to stand proudly alongside other nearby realms. Therefore, I will be asking Golds throughout the realm to report to me on the status of their Copper population, and to offer suggestions for what might best advance the Coppers upon whose strong shoulders our prosperity rests.

He read it to Victory before he sent it in, and she commented, "I see what you are setting out to do. But you cannot stay uncontroversial for long."

"True," he admitted. "But I don't want to start right out by condemning Admirable Silverstones and all he stands for."

"Do you know, he very nearly caused the lynching of two of my best clerks when he was at Ancient Turfrae?" said Victory.

"I can well believe it," said Determined grimly.

The Realm Benefit Party's Secretary of Information, a prematurely balding and greying Silver called Steadfast, was having his daily meeting with the party's leader. Admirable Silverstones, Countygold Upper Hills, was about Determined's age, but heavier-set and with a brisk, decisive air. Steadfast's attention switched constantly between his notepad and his leader's face, looking for his reactions.

The two men were discussing what the newspapers had published that day. The Party had its own official newspaper, called, with more clarity than imagination, *Realm Benefit*. It also had the sympathy of several other, supposedly independent newspapers. The Secretary took quiet pride in his ability to send press releases to the remaining papers that made the Party's point while usually not being so slanted as to be suppressed or ridiculed.

When they came to the topic of the Realmgold's new column, Steadfast wrinkled his brow.

"Education of the Coppers," he said, "would be bad for our cause. Educated people are more difficult to steer."

"You didn't study at the College of Ancient Turfrae," said Admirable. "Educated people are just as easy to steer, you just have to go about it differently. More appeal to pride and less to anger, in general, though you can get them very angry if you know how. But actually, I think this is an opportunity."

"How so?"

"Because it means we can offer to start our own schools. And once you have Coppers sitting in a classroom, with an ideologically pure teacher up front..."

"Yes," said Steadfast, smiling. Not only was it a brilliant idea in and of itself, but it would fall to Steadfast to organize it, meaning his power within the Party would increase.

And if the Party wasn't about power, he didn't know what it was about.

Chapter 5: Mindmagic

Victory's little book arrived the following afternoon with Thorn White.

Like the copy of the Red General's book that Victory had given Determined at their first meeting (which he had now located, and was rereading carefully), it had a personal note on the flyleaf in her fine Elvish hand. This one read, "To my ally Determined, who I hope will also become a friend, from Victory." The title page read *Beginning Exercises for Attaining Command of Oneself.*

Unlike the first book, though, it was not printed. It continued in the same Elvish handwriting, switching from Pektal, the language humans spoke in Denning and Koskant, to an archaic Elvish. It was short, just a couple of chapters, and described several exercises to practice for calm and self-control. Despite his greater interest in history, Determined held the carved blackwood bangle of a mage-minor in mindmagic from the College of Ancient Turfrae, and the exercises looked straightforward.

He thanked her for the gift when they spoke on the farviewer that evening.

"Having read the exercises, and tried the first one out," he said, "I can understand how you always seem so calm. I remember from when I first met you and saw how you work. You speak quietly and unhurriedly, and always, always politely, and yet I swear if you said to one of your people, 'I wonder, would you be so good as to take the Dragonpeak Mountains and move them into the Gulf of Koskant, please,' they would say, 'Of course, Realmgold,' and go and do it."

"Oh, no," said Victory seriously. "They wouldn't say that."

"No?"

"No, they know better than that. They'd ask first if I wanted them moved whole or in pieces."

He looked at her, not sure if she was joking, for a full two heartbeats before she smiled.

"Seriously, though," he said, "is there more than what's in this booklet?"

She didn't answer him immediately, but looked at the floor. As he watched her, he saw an odd transformation come over her. It was like watching someone shrink without actually changing size. She looked up at him again, and he saw a small woman, rather ordinary-looking, dressed simply and with tired eyes.

"What..." he began.

"When I was ten years old," she said, in a voice that was now only quiet, not quiet and authoritative, "I found a book in our manor's library, in the old Elvish section — the books from Empire times. It had fallen down the back of the shelf behind some dull old stuff, and nobody had ever noticed it before. It was a manuscript book, anonymous, in a beautiful clear Elvish hand, and written on the flyleaf was the title:

Methods and Techniques to Attain Command of Oneself and Others. It had graded exercises. That small booklet I sent you contains the most basic of them."

She took a breath, and it was as if she was breathing her authority back into herself and becoming the Realmgold again. "I have practiced those exercises daily for 25 years."

"It's all mindmagic?"

"There is mindmagic of various kinds, yes." She was all the way back to the Realmgold now. "I believe it may include what is referred to in some ancient Elvish writings as 'glamour', as well."

"You... before, you let it drop?"

"Yes."

"I... you looked completely ordinary. I might have passed you on the street." He thought for a moment, too late, and added quickly, "I mean, I wouldn't have recognized you as the Realmgold. You still look..."

She smiled, and waved his babbling away. "I sometimes put on a dark suit, drop the glamour, and walk around the streets observing the life of the people, and how they act when they don't know the Realmgold is looking at them. Nobody has ever said a word to me or given me a second glance."

"Is it difficult?"

"Yes. It takes constant focus, and I grow rather weary of it sometimes." She let the glamour go again and looked at him.

"You actually seem smaller," he said.

"I am small," she said. "But most of the time, nobody notices."

"Victory," he said carefully, "would it be all right — could

I get to know you a little — like this?"

"I'd like that," she said, and smiled. "Perhaps I can get to know myself better as well. It's been lonely, having nobody I can speak to as an equal. I've come to value my conversations with you."

"So have I. I trusted and admired you from the first time we met. Oh, I just realized — was that…?"

She smiled. "The glamour may have helped. But like all mindmagic, it can only assist what is there naturally and make it stronger. It's probably the power of the treaty, more than the power of the glamour, working to help us trust each other as allies."

"You trust me?"

"I do. I think you have great potential. And I am seldom wrong about such things."

On the first Threeday in the second shift-round of Late Harvest, Victory wasn't at her farviewer when Determined tuned in. She had never been late before, and he realized anew how much he'd come to expect, and enjoy, their daily talks.

She wasn't like anyone he'd ever met before. At the College of Ancient Turfrae he had been part of a group of youths who talked philosophy, of course, but it had all been theoretical, and a good bit of it had been dominance games disguised as intellectual argument. Victory was, if anything, more intelligent than any of his old debating partners, but she was concerned with practicalities. What actually *worked* to make people's lives better and the realm stronger? That, he decided, was Victory's constant question. And since it was a question he himself wanted the answer to…

The magic mirror cleared, and showed him the familiar

sight of Victory seating herself in her private tea room.

"My apologies," she said. "I have had a busy evening, and it is far from over yet. But I wanted to give you a warning of what we are doing here, because it will impact you."

"Yes?" he said.

"I have been working with my lawyers on the matter of gnomeservice. You are familiar with the term?"

"It's what the dwarves call their system of managing the work of their gnomes, isn't it?"

"That would be one definition. What I am about to publish tonight, though, is a clarifying law which gives it a different and more accurate definition. I am defining gnomeservice as what it is, which is slavery."

"Slavery?" he said, with a sharp lift to his voice. "That would make it illegal."

All humans were descended from slaves who had been brought, legend said, from another world by the ancient elves. When the Elven Empire had fallen, they had freed themselves — or, by some accounts, vice versa. He had often passed the stone column in the old marketplace of Turfrae, the ancient elven capital, which commemorated the creation, shortly after the Empire's fall, of the Code of Willing. This legal code, the foundation of every civilized human nation's laws, declared slavery of any kind illegal.

"Yes, exactly. I am freeing the gnomes tonight. Any gnome outside a legally constituted dwarf hold, where of course dwarf law is in force, will be able to choose his or her employer and negotiate fair wages and conditions."

"But that's... the dwarves will be furious."

"I would imagine so," said Victory, her voice as calm as ever.

"Won't that lead to economic chaos?"

"A certain amount. But you know what the Red General says…"

"Chaos favors the prepared. You are prepared?"

"As prepared as I can be. I am sorry that I couldn't give you more warning, but I have had to keep this very close."

"Of course. Victory… why now?"

"You don't ask why in general?"

"Well, that seems obvious. It's the right thing to do. And I assume, having got to know you a little lately, that you also have other reasons, that it will advance your plans in some way."

"The gnomes are an enormous skilled labour force, and I need one. At the moment, to get access to them I have to go through the dwarves, who are old-fashioned and slow-moving and inclined to argue every little point. It is like having a lake full of water and a pipe as thick as your finger. I want direct access to gnome labour, and freeing the gnomes — besides being, as you say, the right thing to do — will give it to me."

"I thought there must be some angle. What do you think the dwarves will do?"

"They will probably shut us out as much as they can, though they will not break their sworn contracts, of course. The New Dwarf movement may even welcome the move. I know that they have been arguing for a long time that gnomes will work better if they have more stake in their own labour."

"Do you think there'll be violence?" he asked.

"Probably not against us. Dwarves are used to getting what they want through economic means, and hiring people to fight for them, and I don't think the centaurs, for example, will accept orders to fight against a human realm. Against bandits, certainly, but not legitimate authorities. The centaurs are a law-abiding people. But according to my gnome advisor, there may be fighting inside the dwarfholds. He thinks some of his people will side with the dwarves, out of fear or misplaced loyalty, while others have been waiting for generations for just this opportunity, and may be out for some revenge. It will be a difficult transition, at best."

"Well, good luck with it. When you say it will impact me, though..."

"The gnomes in Denning will hear of it. The dwarves, too. And so will the Human Purity faction. You will have to decide whether you follow me, and if you do, there will be a cost."

"I see," he said, and pursed his lips. "I'll have to think about that."

"The longer you think, the more time they will all have to prepare."

"Quite. Thank you for letting me know, Victory."

"It was the least I could do. And, in fact, I cannot do much more — unless you have something very urgent to talk to me about, I need to get back to coordinating things."

"No, nothing urgent. Well, other than what you've just said, of course."

"Then I shall bid you good night. I hope you get more sleep than I expect to."

Chapter 6: Speeches in the Plaza

The following evening, the evening of what the Koskander press was calling Gnome Day, Victory somehow found time to speak with Determined briefly over the farviewer.

"Thank you for the warning last night," he said. "I've already had a delegation from the dwarves."

"What did you tell them?"

"I said that I would study the matter and let them know," he admitted, dropping his eyes.

"You need to move quickly," she said.

"I know," he said miserably. "The longer I give them, the more they can stockpile supplies and stretch out the confrontation."

"Exactly," she said. "Well, I have to go. It is a busy day here, as you can probably imagine."

"Let me be clear," Countygold Admirable thundered from the steps of the Lakeside Koslin Public Library - a favorite spot for speakers, as it faced onto a large plaza. "Slavery is wrong — for *humans*, because humans are the highest form, the natural inheritors of the world. For lesser races like gnomes, slavery is the only appropriate state. It's not for nothing, my friends, not for nothing that these pale, undersized creatures have been the slaves of the dwarves, themselves a degenerate race, time out of mind. Slavery is their proper condition, and in seeking to change that, the Southerner has unleashed the whirlwind. And if we do not want that wind to sweep us all away, we must resist! Resist any declaration of freedom for the degenerate, of rights for the inferior, of status for the lowest. Resist to our last breath, for we are human, we are the inheritors, we alone have purity."

"Purity!" cried the crowd.

Determined's heart sank as he read the next morning's edition of the *Eye*. It reported Admirable's speech in full. The editorial, signed by Localgold Abundance Northroad, who owned the newspaper, said, "It seems to have become a rule of popular speaking that whatever is repeated often enough, loudly enough and with sufficient passion is regarded as true, even if it is supported by no facts whatsoever…"

Well said, thought Determined, and suddenly his fear was matched by anger. He leaped to his feet, circled his desk, and began to pace back and forth across the rug.

As a student of history, he knew the contributions that non-humans had made to human culture. Most high culture was directly inherited from the elves, and much of the material and technological culture humans possessed came directly from the dwarves. Human Purity was historical nonsense, and for that reason alone he opposed it.

"But that's not enough," he muttered. "One thing to say it's not true. But Victory's right, if we're going to make a better future it's with the help of the dwarves and gnomes and the rest. We'd be cutting off our right arm if we exclude them. What's Silverstones thinking?"

He paced back and forth a couple more times, considering power and wealth.

"If he seizes the wealth of the dwarves, he's well-positioned to take the realm," he concluded. "He doesn't care that in the long term it will harm us all. He only wants power now, and he is *not* a man who will use it responsibly."

He crossed the room again, more slowly.

"So the question is, do I let him take it without a fight?"

He hadn't wanted to be Realmgold, and he didn't think he was much good at it. Perhaps someone who did want it would do a better job, even if it was Silverstones.

"But that's not what Victory thinks," he said aloud, as he stopped at his desk. "She thinks I can make this realm my skyhorse. And if there's one thing I know about Victory, it's that the people she chooses get the job done.

"Reliable!" he bellowed. His secretary's light footsteps hurried to the door separating their offices, and the man peered tentatively round the doorway.

"Reliable, have a proclamation made... no, Nine curse it, this is important enough that I'll do it myself. Announce that I will be speaking on the library steps this afternoon. Invite the newspapers, and the representatives of the dwarves who have been pushing me for a decision. Anyone else can come if they like — don't make a big secret of it. Put up posters, if you want."

"What time this afternoon, Realmgold?"

"At the tenth deep bell. No, the ninth, that will give the papers more time for the evening editions. Go!"

The secretary went off like a rabbit, and Determined circled his desk again, sat, seized a pen and some paper and began to scribble furiously.

By the time he stood at the podium on the library steps, his anger had cooled - and so had something lodged in his gut, because it felt as if he'd swallowed a snowball.

He looked across the crowd. It consisted mostly of Coppers with a few Silver merchants, an Asterist scholar in a three-cornered hat, a lawyer in her shoulder-width round poncho, and a mixed bag of newswriters and their imagetakers at the front. While the square was far from being packed with citizens, they were considerably more numerous than he'd anticipated, and for a moment he wanted to back down and hand his speech to Reliable. Then he thought of Victory's serious dark eyes and her calm daring, swallowed hard and began.

"I have not stood here to address you often," he said. "But today I have an announcement that I very much want to identify myself with. I do not want to deliver it through a messenger or in a press release passed from office to newspaper. I want to bring it to you in person.

"You will have heard, of course, how our southern neighbors have declared that gnomeservice, as practiced by the dwarves, is the same as slavery and therefore illegal under the most ancient human laws. You have heard mixed accounts, no doubt, of price instability, of prospects for increasing prosperity as humans also begin to employ gnomes, of economic struggles between the dwarves and the Realm of

Koskant — which the Realm of Koskant, incidentally, is well positioned to win.

"Some of you have heard from these very steps an argument — no, not an argument, a mere unsupported assertion — that the gnomes deserve their state of subjugation, that it is the natural order, simply because it has been the case for so long. I reject that assertion utterly."

There was silence for long enough for Determined's heart to beat twice. He knew this, because he could feel it thumping against his ribs.

"I am announcing now that I am joining our friends, neighbors and long-time allies in Koskant in recognizing the injustice that has long been perpetrated against the gnomes. Here, today, now, I am proclaiming in the same words as Realmgold Victory that slavery includes all compelled labour without pay, that gnomeservice is clearly slavery, and that, according to our most ancient code of laws, it is and always has been illegal in this realm."

The dwarves gathered to one side of the plaza began to protest, and he raised his voice above them. "As Victory did, I am also proclaiming amnesty for past abuses, but from this moment, all gnomes outside a legally constituted dwarf hold must consider themselves free agents, free to take employment with whomever they wish at whatever wage they may freely negotiate and under the same conditions as any human worker. Lacking Koskant's useful corps of Gryphon Clerks, I am not in a position to have dwarf holds inspected and certified free from slavery, but as soon as I am in such a position I will institute the further condition that all goods sold or transported in Denning from a dwarf hold within Denning must be so certified. I will not tolerate slavery in my

Realm, and I will not tolerate blind prejudice either. It is through freedom and equality for *all* within the Realm that we will build a prosperous Denning.

"Thank you, that is all. Any questions are to be addressed through my secretary." He indicated Reliable, standing to his left.

He stepped down from the podium, and the crowd erupted. A few were cheering, more were yelling abuse. Scuffles broke out, and the guards who had been casually standing at the edges of the square moved in. Other guards hurried him up the steps and into the library, then through a side door to an unmarked steam carriage.

"I've done it now," he said, to himself, but one of the guards responded.

"Yes, Realmgold." The man's eyes held a respect that Determined had not seen there before.

Chapter 7: The Red General's List

Victory listened with her usual calm demeanor that evening as Determined described his day.

"Congratulations," she said. "What decided you?"

"I just couldn't stand by and let that fool rant out his lies any longer," he said.

She considered him carefully.

"There is more to it than that, I think," she said. Her glamour was down, as usual when they spoke now, and that evidence of trust made it hard for him not to be candid.

Determined sighed, and looked down. "There's a history between us," he admitted.

"I am always interested in history."

He pursed his lips, thinking. "All right," he said. "The Countygold of Upper Hills and I were at the College of Ancient Turfrae at the same time. Actually he was there first, he's a couple of years older. By the time I started, he was already establishing himself as an important leader in the Human Purity movement, which had begun a few years before with a small group of professors and students. Simply a theoretical thing at first. Silverstones — as he was then, he hadn't inherited the County yet — took it and made it a movement."

He flushed, and rubbed the back of his neck. "There was a girl I wanted to get to know, and I heard her say to a friend of hers that she was going to one of his meetings, so I went along, hoping, you know... And I didn't see her, but I listened to him speak. He was good. Brilliant, really. Inspirational. In those days he was more subtle, his arguments were more sophisticated, tuned, I suppose, to his audience. I started going regularly, and he took notice of me, cultivated me. In retrospect it was obviously because I was related to the Realmgold, but at the time he made it seem like it was for me, myself, that he respected me and valued me. He was good at that. He did it with everyone who he thought he could use, more or less, but I didn't pay attention to that. I... I became a follower. A passionate one. I was looking for meaning in history, some overarching story, and Silverstones and his group provided it. And I was looking for a group to belong to, as well, one that made me feel like what I did and said and thought was important.

"At that time a lot of the history faculty were starting to come over to a Human Purity line. But there was one professor, an older man, near retirement. He was my favorite teacher, because he made everything so interesting and vivid. He would take us walking around Ancient Turfrae and describe things that had happened in the places where we stood, and you could almost imagine they were happening in front of you. I still remember his lecture in front of the Column of Willing practically word for word.

"Anyway, he had always stayed quiet on Human Purity, for or against. His great work was a translation of an old Elvish book. He'd spent twenty years on it. And one day I arrived in his office for a tutorial, and he was excited. He'd been working on his translation, and he'd found, he said, evidence that when the elves had brought us, humans, to this world, they'd changed us somehow so that we could do magic."

"Interesting," said Victory. "They would certainly have been capable of something like that, from all I've read."

"Yes, they would. Both technically and morally. But of course the first thing I seized on was what that would mean for Human Purity. It would mean not only that we weren't pure, but that nonhumans had shaped us, made us what we are."

"I suppose I can see that. You argued?"

"I was an insufferable little snot, if you call that arguing. Ended up storming out and going straight to Silverstones."

"What did he say?"

"Thanked me for drawing it to his attention."

Determined shifted uncomfortably in his chair and ran his hands through his hair, then squeezed them together. "The next day, there was a fire in the professor's rooms."

"His translation?"

"Yes, and the Elvish original. But he came in unexpectedly, and *somehow* he hit his head, and... Well, between that and the smoke... He was an old man."

"They murdered him?" Victory's usual calm tone held a hint of emotion.

"It may not have been completely deliberate. But yes."

They were both silent for several heartbeats, then she

asked, "What did you do?"

"Went and confronted Silverstones. He heard me out, and then said one of his prefabricated ideological phrases, something about purifying academic understanding or some such nonsense. I felt the most powerful desire to throttle him that I've ever felt for anyone, but he had these two big 'friends' who always went around with him, and… all the blood rushed to my head, and then it drained away again, and I turned around and left without a word. I was furious. Really, genuinely furious, not just fanatically worked up like I had been with the professor."

"You broke with him?"

"I did, and I started talking to people I'd noticed were less than completely on board with his program, the ones who stayed quiet and avoided the question. Because if you spoke up you got… harassed. I saw it happen, but up until then I'd thought it was the right thing. Driving out the ideologically impure, the ones who didn't understand like *we* did."

"Did you get very far?"

"Everyone was afraid. Most of them wouldn't even talk to me. I think they thought I was working for Silverstones, trying to get them to incriminate themselves so they could be persecuted. The death of the professor had shaken everyone. And then, before I could do much more, or rather before his hulking 'friends' got round to coming to my rooms and grinding me into the rug, my uncle died and I was summoned back to Lakeside Koslin for the family vote. And of course I never went back."

"And you have been keeping watch on him in the five years since."

"Yes, though I've not spoken out publicly until today."

"But now you have drawn the line, and unfortunately he will feel obligated to step across it."

"Yes, he will, won't he? But he would have sooner or later."

"Correct. And now he is not as ready as he would have been, and you have taken action which he must respond to, instead of the other way around. That is good.

"Now, what I hope is that people will quietly or publicly contact you with messages of support, now that you have identified yourself as standing against the bigots. When they do, I want you to give them these." She held up a small device.

"What's that?"

"The latest thing from my clever man, Dignified Printer. I asked him if it would be cheaper and simpler to create devices that only sent the voice instead of a voice and an image, and this is what he came up with. Half the trick of managing him is asking the right questions."

"It's a voice sender?"

"Yes, and a child can assemble it out of a few wires, a cheap crystal and a bit of etched copper, plus some simple dials. Costs copper anvils rather than silver hammers. I will send you the design and a template for the sigils, plus a few examples."

"I suppose I will need to find a manufactory I can trust."

"Judging by what happened here, you will soon have the gnomes to staff one of your own. Find an empty building that is well-protected and has somewhere for them to live, and move them in there quietly."

"So these devices will help us stay in touch and make plans against the RBP? What if they get hold of one? Won't they be able to listen in?"

"Ah, that is one of the clever parts. You see these?" She held up the device at a different angle so that he could see the set of eight dials, each marked with the Dwarvish numerals for 0 to 15. "Two devices are only in sympathy when their dials are set to the same code, and since there are more than four billion possible codes, that provides practical security as well as allowing multiple conversations at a time. Also, you can leak some of the codes deliberately and mislead them." She sounded almost childlike in her enthusiasm for a moment, a side of Victory he hadn't previously seen.

"You're enjoying this, aren't you?"

"Oh, I love being one step ahead. Or more. Now, let us go through the Red General's List."

Determined knew that one. He had been carefully rereading the Red General, an ancient elven military man who had risen from the Copper class to the imperial throne by his excellent grasp of how to make the most of situations. Determined had used simple mental techniques to memorize some of the more interesting contents.

"All right, um, allies. I've got you, and hopefully other people who will contact me now. In fact, I've already had some quiet and subtle indications of approval from some of my guards and one or two Golds."

"Excellent. What's next?"

"Intelligence. I have some intelligencers who I'm confident are loyal, and I'm already having them check the others for any links to the RBP. I'll issue them with the voice senders, too, as soon as I have them."

"Good. What else?"

"Logistics and supply. I'll want my own network that

can't be compromised easily by the RBP — there are a few big merchants who are RBP supporters, presumably because they think they'll win, so I need to be able to work around them. Having some gnomes loyal to me who will make me things will help."

"Correct," said Victory.

"Then there's, um, troops. Again, the intelligencers will need to check the loyalty of key officers. I don't want to ask openly for loyalty vows just yet, it would let Silverstones know too much. My personal guard are all Salvanusmouth mercenaries, of course, so they should be safe enough."

"I would count civilians as troops as well, if they are supporters. Especially if they are organized."

"That's true. He'll certainly be using civilians. All right, what does that leave? Plans?"

"Plans."

"A plan for attack, a plan for defense, a plan for withdrawal, and a plan for when the other plans fail," he said.

"Right."

"Attack, well, there are a few parts to that. Winning the hearts of the people, educating them, building alliances with the Golds, and discrediting the RBP."

"Watch out for discrediting, that can be a pipe with two ends. Though I am sure they are already thinking of ways to discredit you."

"I'm sure they are too. How do you handle your Tried and True Party, by the way?"

"I ignore them, mostly, to be honest with you. I do not think you can compare them to your RBP. The Tried and Trues disagree with my methods and objectives, and some of them are unpleasant people and some of them are ruthless, but mostly within the law. The RBP are after power at any cost, particularly at any cost that is borne by people other than them."

"True. Which is why I can't keep ignoring them. All right, that's attack — anything to add?"

"No, that is exactly what I would do, in fact have done. You have to look better than the alternative."

"In the case of the RBP you wouldn't think that would be difficult."

"No, but hate is a very powerful force."

"That's true. All right, a plan for defense. Guards, obviously. I'm going to be more careful about speaking in public like I did today."

"Do you have a personal shield?" she asked.

"Of course, though it's an old one. I think it was my grandfather's. It makes a buzzing noise in my ears, so I hate wearing it, but I'll wear it when I'm out of the palace."

"Good. What about defense for your open supporters?"

"I'll do what I can. If there are very many of them it'll be hard, though."

"Mention defense to them. They know their own resources best."

"I will. Anything else?"

"Warn the dwarves and gnomes. I am sure the dwarves are probably not listening at the moment, but warn the gnomes. I can provide channels through my gnomes here if you need them."

"Thanks. I will need that. Now, withdrawal."

"Do you want one of my skyboats?" offered Victory.

Determined, taken aback, looked at her speechlessly. The Koskander skyboats were the fastest thing in the air, and his

51

military lusted after them like a schoolboy.

"Are you serious?"

"My dear Determined, we are allies. I am happy to lend you a skyboat on the understanding that you will not have it taken to pieces to see how it works. Not that any dwarves would probably do that for you just at the moment."

"Then... then I accept. Thank you, Victory. I owe you... everything."

"A little less than everything. But it is of no account. I will probably want something you can give me someday, you know, and we can discuss it then. Now, have you given any thought to a plan for when the other plans fail?"

"Not so far."

"So, your attacks have been repelled, your defenses are breached and you cannot escape. What do you do?"

"Well, I could abdicate in favor of my heir, if I had one. But I don't. My cousins are a mediocre bunch, nothing much to pick between them, and they still hate each other just as much as when I was elected."

"Interesting. So there would be succession issues if you were killed?"

"Some, though I'm sure the family would work them out. It's not as complex here as your system of electing the Realmgold from among the Provincegolds, though I'm sure that has its advantages."

"Hmm. Well, we will just have to make sure you can escape, that there are always a couple of clear routes to the skyboat — perhaps I had better lend you more than one. Because make no mistake, Determined, there is every chance that you will have to use that plan before we are finished here."

"That's rather sobering."

"It is, but let us not live in a dream. The RBP is growing in support, and even if they only capture one person in eight or one person in sixteen to their side, they are a danger. I am very much afraid that civil war is on the horizon for Denning, though I will do everything I can to help you prevent it."

Determined bit his lip. How had she talked him into this? His realm about to be plunged into civil war, his own life in danger…

He squared his shoulders. All of that would have come in any case. But at least by opposing it he could retain some self-respect.

Chapter 8: Less Than Admirable

Admirable was silent for far too long after Steadfast brought him the news of Determined's speech and his emancipation of the gnomes. Steadfast could feel the pressure building, like it did before one of the violent storms that blew in from the Inland Sea and wrecked fishing boats in late harvest. Admirable's expression tightened, and his face gradually darkened. Steadfast felt like a man on the edge of a cliff when the ground under his feet suddenly slumps.

"You assured me," said Admirable quietly, but with a roughness to his tone, "that the Realmgold was isolated and harmless."

"I was wrong," said Steadfast, just as quietly.

Admirable leapt to his feet and pounded the desk between them. He looked as if he was ready to leap over it and go for Steadfast's throat, and the Secretary of Information took an involuntary step backwards, stumbling against the chair in which he had not been invited to sit.

"You were wrong!" Admirable bellowed, foam flying

from his lips. "You were wrong! Do you have any idea what you have done here? Our entire government strategy was based on Determined not living up to his name, because you assured me that the man had lost whatever spine he might have once had. Well, he has apparently found a new one somewhere at the back of all his bookshelves!"

Admirable slumped heavily back into his chair. "Tell me," he said, once again quiet, "that you have a backup plan."

"I... I... I..." stammered Steadfast.

"You were wrong and you had no backup plan!" screamed his leader. He leaned forward and pointed a forefinger at Steadfast, quivering with rage. "We are caught on the wrong foot, we are running round like ants, do you have any idea?"

"I... forgive me, Leader."

"Forgive you." He was back to menacingly quiet again, but it lasted only for the two words. "Forgive you? You moron, you have ruined plans years in the making! Do you have any appreciation of what I have sacrificed, how I have worked, what depends on this?"

The excoriation lasted more than twenty minutes. Steadfast emerged, backwards, with his ears burning, and blinking tears from his eyes. He hadn't cried since he was ten years old.

The three people in the outer office busied themselves on pieces of paper with extreme focus as he stumbled past.

When he was safely outside, Steadfast wiped his tears (and his leader's spittle) from his face, took a deep breath, and headed for his office. He didn't know how he was going to turn this around, but he would do it if it killed him. Because, he reflected, not doing it would probably kill him, no metaphor involved.

Admirable was an early riser, and their clash occurred not long after dawn. By sunset, Steadfast had drafted his leader's next speech. It took all the focus he had left, after an exhausting day, not to fidget from foot to foot as Admirable silently, and without looking up, read it through. The only sound in the office was the occasional, unhurried turn of a page.

Finally, he met Steadfast's eyes and said, coldly, "It will do." He turned back to the first page and started reading it again, this time reaching for a pen to make edits.

"Go," he said, without looking up.

Steadfast went.

Next afternoon, in front of the library, Admirable spoke to a packed crowd. The word had gone around, and aristocratic supporters of the Realm Benefit Party had sent their Coppers along. Spaced regularly around the crowd were an unusually large number of members of the RBP's Special Security Group, large men in dark-grey coats that reached to their shins, leaning on long wooden staves.

Tight-jawed, with flashing eyes and flourishing gestures, Admirable began to speak. He spoke of the greatness of Denning, the pride of its people, its enviable history and national character. The crowd was soon with him, and roared with approval at all the right moments. He worked up to a shout, which had them cheering for a good 20 or 30 heartbeats. Then he raised his hands. The crowd quieted.

"You may have heard," he said, quietly enough that his hearers had to strain forward to hear him, "that Denning's future greatness will be very different from this. You may have heard, from a bookish, pale man blinking in the unaccustomed sun, that Denning's future greatness will be based on education and learning. You may have heard, from a puppet of the south" — by now he was building his voice up again — "that Denning's future greatness will come from learning from elves, and dwarves, and gnomes, and welcoming them into partnership as equals. But I say no!" He thundered out this last sentence suddenly. "I say that our greatness comes not from what we know, but from who we are. We are Denningers. We are pure humans. We do not need the knowledge of corrupt, degenerate lesser races, and we do not want them among us, infecting our children with their degenerate, corrupted ways. We are free! And we will continue to be free, and we will continue to be great, as we resist with the strength of our arms and with our very lives, giving our last breath to advance pure humanity! Purity!"

With the last, shouted word, his hand came down upon the lectern, even as the staves of the Special Security Group, in a coordinated moment, came down on the cobbles of the square.

"Purity!" cried the crowd.

"You know what he has just done?" asked Victory, as she and Determined discussed the speech that evening. "He has deliberately set out to recruit stupid people. If we cannot defeat that, we should just give up and join him."

"Unfortunately," said Determined wryly, "there are a lot of stupid people."

"Oh, and you know what the Red General says about that," said Victory, with the cheerful enthusiasm of a fan discussing her favorite author.

"Um, don't meet them on an even basis, use their numbers against them, and... is that the Nine Factors part?"

Victory began quoting, in the original Elvish. "'The wise commander, seeing a force that has superior numbers, does not despair. Rather, such a commander takes action, refusing to meet the larger force face to face on open ground, and takes steps to use the opponent's numbers to advantage. For there are nine factors of victory to consider, apart from the number of the enemy. These are the factors of location, being terrain, placement and maneuverability; the factors of one's troops, being their condition, training and armament; and the factors of the mind, being tactics, intelligence and attitude. Only when one's opponent is one's equal in all of the nine factors do numbers become insuperable.'"

"Do you know the whole thing by heart?" he asked, when she finished.

"Oh, no," she said. "Chapters three and five are quite boring. I don't bother with those. Now, have you started making those farspeakers yet?"

That night, a tall man in a bulky, hooded cloak strode down a dark alley near the centre of Gulfport. Backing up against a stone panel, part of the wall of an anonymous building, he knocked in a deliberate pattern.

The stone panel shifted aside, and he vanished into the passageway within.

At the other end of the passageway, a much bulkier, and more brightly-dressed, figure waited in a heavy gilded chair, in a room deliberately lit to create shadows everywhere except for where he sat at the focus of several lights. The figures of retainers or guards lurked in those shadows. The man in the chair wore an elaborately-embroidered waistcoat, dripping with gold braid, a shirt with puffed and slashed sleeves, puff-leg trousers and hand-tooled leather boots with serpentine gilded patterns, in the style popular under the previous Realmgold.

The cloaked man bowed, and said only, "Gold." The seated figure nodded heavily to him.

"What do you want?" he asked.

"My master would... appreciate some help with a project." Certain vowels of the man's speech betrayed an origin in Denning.

"Say more," said the Gold.

"It would be convenient to my master if there were demonstrations in Gulfport in support of his convictions."

"Marches in the streets, that sort of thing?"

"Exactly, Gold. Exactly. And we are under the impression that you would be able to arrange something of the kind."

The Gold regarded him levelly for a heartbeat, and then said, "Your impression is correct."

"We appreciate that certain expenses will be involved," continued the Denninger, producing a bag which made a soft clinking noise. The Gold made a gesture that didn't quite dismiss the bag, but suggested that politeness dictated the Denninger should discreetly place it on a table in the shadows, out of sight. He did this, and, straightening up, said, "There will be a personal advertisement in the *Gulfport Herald*, to Purity from her friend A., with the usual code to specify when and where the first demonstration should take place.

Afterwards, I will contact you again. Acceptable?"

The Gold gave an abrupt nod, and the Denninger, without a further word, bowed himself out and retreated along the passage. The door was not visibly attended, so he checked at a sliding panel which allowed him to see, through a prism, if there was anyone in the alley outside.

There was not, and he released the latch and slipped out into the night.

Two days later, a motley collection of Coppers, mostly wearing some bit of dark-grey rag to show allegiance to the RBP, marched along the Grand Parade, the main street of Gulfport, parallel to the river. They chanted Human Purity slogans and waved their fists in the air, occasionally breaking off to smash a dwarf business's window.

Low bars along the waterfront did a good trade that evening, and many of the patrons still displayed their rags.

The Head Clerk of the Realmgold's Agents reported to Victory that many of the marchers had been identified as suspected members of criminal gangs. She nodded, as if she had expected this information.

"And what is your plan?" she asked.

"Work the usual informants," the Head Clerk said. "Follow the money. That's all we can do."

The Realmgold nodded and the Head Clerk strode off, her pale Victory suit making a swish-swish noise as her thighs rubbed together.

Chapter 9: Ambush

A small dwarf caravan wound its dusty way towards the Thunder Gorge dwarfhold in the northwest of Denning. Its members, six mules, four gnomes, the dwarf in charge, and a centaur guard, had pushed hard to get to the hold before dark, but they weren't quite going to achieve it. The night was drawing in, and the mules would soon be stumbling on rough patches of the poorly-maintained road.

The small caravan's centaur guard was known, like all centaur caravan guards, as Muscles, though his given name was Tree. He looked away to preserve his vision as Pack of Sevenhills, the dwarf, lit the travel-globes on each beast's harness, assisted by his gnome leader, Pot.

Muscles was picturing being beside a warm fire with a drink in his hand and out of his leather barding when he heard a ruckus from up the road. He came alert despite his weariness, and quickly strung his bow, then held it low by his side.

"Just drunken locals, by the sound," said Pack.

"Maybe," said Muscles. "I'm taking no chances. Things are going to get ugly down here at some point."

Rounding a corner, they came upon a small mob of humans. They showed signs, as Pack had said, of drunkenness, but the light of burning torches mingled with the yellowish magical light of Pack's travel-globes, and there were a surprising number of farm implements for the time of evening.

"Well," said a human near the front of the group, "what have we here?"

"Looks like de-gen-e-rates," slurred one of his companions, who was eyeing the mules and their burdens.

"Three-fingered degenerates and a half-beast," agreed the first. "What do you say, boys?"

"Purity!" shouted the mob raggedly, waving their farm implements.

"Let's get them!" the second human cried out, and they fanned out and began a ragged charge, chanting "Pu-ri-ty, pu-ri-ty" and lowering their implements like spears or raising them like swords, depending on the length of the shaft.

Muscles' bow came up, an arrow from the quiver on his back met it, and he drew and fired in less time than it takes to blink. The first speaker, apparently the leader, fell with a cry, Muscles' shaft protruding from his left shoulder. Almost before he hit the ground, his yes-man got the same treatment.

A couple of nearby humans faltered, seeing their two spokesmen fall. One took to his heels, and the other stumbled back and fell on his buttocks with a grunt, then, after a moment, started crawling away. Most of them, though, were too fixated on their attack to notice (and too drunk).

A third human fell to an arrow — a big man with a reasonably sharp pickaxe — before the six who hadn't yet fallen or fled reached the little caravan.

Muscles reared, and gave his war cry. He had trained the mules well, and they swapped end-for-end and began to kick out at their attackers. One, propelled by hooves, flew through the air like a sack full of straw, struck the ground heavily and lay still. Another, faced with Muscles' own hooves windmilling in his face, covered his eyes with his forearms and stumbled backwards, where he tripped over the big man's body and fell down. He continued to cower as Muscles hauled his broadsword from its straps on his back, next to his quiver, and decapitated a hayfork. The hayfork's wielder dropped it hurriedly and began backing away.

The fight had lasted perhaps sixteen heartbeats so far, and eight of the eleven were out of action. The remaining three, though, had surrounded the little knot of unarmed gnomes gathered around Pack and were beating on them with their implements. Pot fell, bleeding from his head.

Muscles bellowed, sounding more like a bull than a stallion, but there was a mule bucking between him and the gnomes. He reached over it with his long, muscular arms and slashed at the shoulder of the nearest man, at the fullest extension of the broadsword. The man blocked clumsily, but effectively, with his mattock, and it clanged.

The startled mule bolted, and Muscles surged forward and swung the flat of his blade from right to left, knocking one man out with the blade itself and a second with the sword's grip and his large hand.

The third, the mattock man, heaved his improvised weapon up above his head preparatory to bringing it down at Muscles' enormous chest. While Muscles appreciated his courage, he didn't appreciate his intent. He caught the mattock on his blade with a thud that shuddered through the human's hands, and kicked him precisely in the solar plexus with a heavy hoof.

Muscles surveyed the area. A couple more humans had fled, several were groaning more or less quietly, and three lay terminally still. The gnomes and Pack were looking stunned, a couple of them literally. Pot was sprawled at Pack's feet, and even before Muscles bent and checked, he knew he wasn't ever getting up again. He sheathed his sword, lifted the gnome and tucked him into one of his empty saddlebags.

"Careful!" said Pack.

"Not much point in being careful with him now, I'm afraid," said Muscles. "Who else is badly hurt?"

There were a couple of broken arms, some bruises and a nasty concussion. Muscles scooped up the concussed gnome, rallied the others and double-timed them, with the remaining mules, in the direction of the dwarf hold. Pack was inclined to protest at leaving one of the mules lost in the darkness, but Muscles was in command under conditions of threat, and the caravan owner was overruled. "We don't have time to look for it," said the centaur. "Either it turns up or not. Our concern now is to get behind stone before those humans come back with reinforcements."

At dawn the next morning, a nervous and hastily-dressed herald in the human Localgold's colors was waiting at the gate of the dwarf hold when it opened.

"You'd better come in," said the gate-dwarf seriously.

That evening, Victory's welcoming smile over the farviewer vanished when she saw Determined's face.

"What's happened?"

"That depends on exactly which report you listen to. Either a mob of RBP supporters or a small group of drunken rural Coppers, or the two in one, attacked a dwarf caravan coming down from the north."

"Casualties?"

"One gnome dead, one badly injured, some other injuries. Three humans dead, five injured, two seriously."

"A dwarf caravan did that?"

"Yes, they had a centaur."

"Ah. Well, that sounds like an RBP attack all right."

"Because of the centaur?"

"Yes, because only RBP followers would be stupid enough to attack a caravan guarded by a centaur."

"True," he said, but he didn't smile at her small joke.

"There's a complication, isn't there," she said.

"There is. The nearest dwarf hold is claiming bloodprice from the Localgold. But the Localgold is counterclaiming. He's an RBP supporter. And neither of them will back down."

"I don't know your laws," she commented, "but here, that would go up to the Countygold next."

"Yes, but she's not an open supporter of either side, and I'm not sure whether she'll rule in favor of the dwarves."

"I suppose we are sure that's the correct decision?"

"I am. I've seen the images, read the accounts — I sent a skycourier as soon as I heard. Some of the humans are saying that the centaur attacked them first, but they're obviously lying."

"So what will you do?"

What, he asked himself, would Victory do herself? He looked down, pondering.

"What I'll do," he said, looking up again, "is get a

farspeaker to the Countygold concerned. Assure her of my moral and practical support. Offer her a few troops for security. Good troops. State my confidence in her evenhandedness, and that I'm sure she will judge the case fairly and announce the verdict to which the evidence leads."

"A good plan. Treat people as if they're trustworthy," she said, "and they'll strive not to disappoint you. Or that, at least, is my experience."

The same cloaked figure met the same Gold in the same shadowed room.

"My master is... displeased," said the Denninger. "The turnout was commendable, and the performance satisfactory, but — as you have no doubt seen — the payoff at the end of the march was spotted by a reporter for the *Koskander* newspaper."

The Gold inclined his head. "The underlings involved have been appropriately chastised," he rumbled.

"Be that as it may, this opens further such demonstrations to the charge of being equally stage-managed. It compromises their effectiveness. Accordingly, we will have to move up Stage 2."

When he did not continue, the Gold gestured at him to do so.

"Stage 2 is a more active confrontation with our ultimate targets, the dwarves and gnomes. And, inevitably, the authorities. Do you have reasonable incendiary skills within your organization?"

The Gold nodded slowly.

"Then here is what my master desires..."

Chapter 10: The Trial

Countygold Constance Blueclay's courtroom had never been so packed. Hers was normally a quiet county, agricultural for the most part, but also a centre for skilled potters and brickmakers who used the eponymous clay to produce useful and beautiful objects.

Now she had had to requisition the Potters' Guildhall to hold a trial that was turning into a carnival of fools.

The newspapers — seemingly all the newspapers — had sent newswriters, who sat at the front of the improvised courtroom. She had banned their imagetakers from the courtroom, but they clustered outside, chewing seed and spitting on the usually pristine brick pavement, and fired the flashing crystals of their dwarfmade imagemaking devices at anyone who came past.

A number of large men in dark grey had come, and she had had the troops that young Determined had sent her take away their staves, check them for other weapons and then admit them. (And then check everyone else for weapons, so as not to show bias.) They were citizens, albeit not of her county, and she had no grounds to exclude them. They sat together at the back, the western wall.

Along the southern wall were a number of serious expressions surrounded by elaborately-woven beards, with a scattering of shorter beards and larger noses — the dwarves and gnomes, respectively, supporting one group of the accused. Along the northern wall were a collection of less-well-kempt beards and patterned headscarves above coarsely-woven Copper tunics, the friends and families of the other group. Denninger law allowed the trials to be combined, since the outcome of each was inextricable from the other.

Down the middle aisle stood twelve of the troops, facing in alternating directions. Constance had pondered whether it was more important not to show obvious suspicion of the RBP's grey men or to watch them, and had decided on the latter, so three soldiers stood behind the dwarves in an area hastily cleared of chairs, facing the RBP. Their weapons were not drawn and they were under instructions to keep their expressions neutral, but be ready to act if trouble started.

Two more soldiers guarded each of the three doors of the hall, one standing inside and one outside. The middle-aged but fit-looking sergeant commanding the squad of 27 stood just in front of the justice bench, to Constance's left, his eyes everywhere. Four more were out the back with the accused, and the last one, a corporal who waited on Constance's right, would fetch each of the accused as they came to testify and guard them while they did so.

Constance checked the clock at the back of the hall and rang her judicial bell. The court speaker called "Order, order," and the low mutter of voices fell silent.

Constance's official judicial table that she used in her usual courtroom had been moved to the platform of the hall.

She stood up behind it, a slight, fiftyish, grey-haired woman who needed the reading glasses that she looked over at the gathered crowd.

Here we go, she thought.

"We are here," she said, "to ascertain the facts about the incident which occurred night before last, just south of Boulder Bend, between a dwarf caravan and a group of local men. I will hear testimony from those who were present and survived, and I will render judgement based on the principles of justice and the law of Denning." She paused and tracked her gaze across the diverse groups. "Anyone who disrupts the proceedings will be ejected without appeal. Is that clear to everybody?"

There were nods from various parts of the hall. The grey-clad RBP men didn't nod, just sat stiffly. There were mutterings among the dwarves, but she chose to assume they were translations being made for those who didn't speak Pektal. The newswriters scribbled, and the Coppers shuffled their feet.

"Good," she said, and sat. "I will have the participants in the incident come in one at a time and give testimony as to what occurred. Call..." she squinted at her notes... "Tree Stonecircle."

The advocate for the Coppers bounced to his feet as if on a spring. His appearance was against him — he was pop-eyed, with a receding chin and advancing teeth — but he was a highly skilled lawyer, too highly skilled for the Coppers to be paying him themselves, thought Constance.

"Advocate Trustworthy," she said, acknowledging him. She thought: Trustworthy, what a name for a lawyer.

"May I inquire of the court why the first witness to be

called is the principal accused?"

"One of the principal accused," she pointed out. "And I am calling him first because, having read through the depositions made by the participants, I concluded that his account gives the fullest outline of the incident. That is not," she said, as he opened his mouth, "a judgement of its accuracy, only of its level of detail." She nodded to the corporal, who had been waiting for her ruling, and he hurried out the back to fetch the centaur.

There was some murmuring among the Coppers when Muscles appeared, which Constance hushed with her bell and a hard glare that said: Remember, I can throw you out. The RBP men sat silently, obviously determined to give her no excuse.

It was the magistrate's prerogative to question the witness first, so she began, once he had been sworn in.

"You are Tree Stonecircle?"

"Yes, Countygold," he said, in a surprisingly tenor voice. His head was about three dwarfpaces above the ground, and, seated, she had to look up at him. He was neatly dressed in the centaur style: a grey tunic cut long at the front and short at the back, and a light-blue outer garment that started out as a cloak and ended up as a horse blanket.

"You may address me as Magistrate while we are in session. You were hired by the dwarf Pack of Sevenhills as a caravan guard?"

"Yes, Magistrate."

She led him through the outline of events, which he recited calmly and clearly, like a military officer giving his report. His enormous hooves stayed planted foursquare on the platform, and he didn't fidget, nor did his speech stumble.

The Trial

She handed him over, as was the tradition, to Trustworthy, who as far as Tree was concerned was acting as the opposing advocate.

Trustworthy leapt to his feet and leaned forward, gesturing up at the centaur. "Tree Stonecircle," he said, "you have testified under court-geis that the humans you killed began the altercation. Is this true?"

"Yes, Advocate," said Tree.

"And does the geis bind you?" he asked.

Tree blinked, at a loss for the first time. "I'm sorry, Advocate, I don't understand," he said.

"Are you bound by your geis in court?"

"Of course I am, Advocate."

"But you're more than half an animal."

Murmurs began on both sides of the court, and Constance rang her bell sharply. "Advocate, I suggest that you desist from this line of questioning," she said. "I am mindmage enough to confirm that the geis does bind the witness to tell the truth, as it does any other witness."

Trustworthy bowed to her unctuously and continued.

"So what was it that led you to conclude that the humans concerned had attacked you?"

"One of them shouted 'let's get them', and they all ran at us with weapons," he said. More than one of the newswriters smirked, and they all scribbled faster.

"And these so-called weapons, of what did they consist?"

"Sharp bits of metal on poles, mostly," he said. One newswriter let out a short laugh, glanced at Constance and fell silent.

"They were, in fact, agricultural tools, were they not? Hayforks, mattocks, scythes and the like?"

"Yes, Advocate. Sharp bits of metal on poles," said Tree.

"They were not, for example, spears and swords?"

"No, Advocate, they were not. I imagine that such items are difficult to obtain for civilians."

"What you imagine is not evidence," said Trustworthy sharply. "So you admit that they were not weapons?"

"No, Advocate, I admit that they were not spears and swords. They were capable of doing harm to us and I judged that that was the intent of the people holding them, which made them weapons. It is my job to make these determinations and act upon them."

"So had they actually laid their implements on you when you shot your bow?"

"No, Advocate. That's rather the point of a bow," said Tree. "You can defend yourself from a distance."

"So you shot — how many?"

"Three, Advocate. After that they were too close."

"And what did you do next? Remind me?"

"I drew my sword and defended myself, my employer, and my fellow employees."

"So you attacked a group of peasants, who had nothing but farm tools to defend themselves, with weapons of war."

"Advocate, I defended myself and my group against an unprovoked attack with improvised weapons. It's my job."

"And you stick to this story."

"I do, Advocate."

"Yours to question," said Trustworthy to the other advocate, a skinny man called Hopeful with a big blade of a nose, and sat down.

Hopeful, a local man whom Constance had worked with often and with whom she swapped seedlings and talked

The Trial

gardening on occasion, stood, straightened his lawyer's shoulder-width black poncho, and asked, "Mister Tree, how many of your opponents were killed in the encounter, do you know?"

"I believe it was three, Advocate."

"And you base this on?"

"Rapid examination at the scene," he said. "It's possible that one or two more may have died afterwards, after I left."

"And how did they die, these three?"

"Two from my shots. The third man I shot, the big one with the pickaxe, looked as if he would live to me. Then one of them was kicked by one of the mules, and he hit pretty hard. Looked like he had internal injuries."

"So the ones you fought with your sword...?"

"One I disarmed by cutting the head off his weapon. Two I knocked out with the flat of the blade. The last one I kicked, but he should have survived all right."

"So you had a sword, but you didn't stab anyone with it."

"Broadsword, Advocate. Not really a stabbing weapon."

"You didn't cut anyone, then."

"No, Advocate."

"Why was that?"

"I try not to kill people if I can avoid it."

"Thank you, Mister Tree," said Hopeful, and sat down.

"Thank you, Mister Tree," echoed Constance, "that will be all. The court," she said to the room at large, "has seen documentation which shows that the centaur Tree Stonecircle is a licensed caravan guard, permitted to carry and use weapons in defense of his employer and his employer's goods." She paused, looked down at her notes, and said, "Call Root Pinegrove."

The corporal led Tree back into the back room on Constance's left, emerged, ducked into the back room on her right and brought out a medium-sized Copper who walked rather carefully, as if in pain. His heavy breathing was clearly audible in the courtroom, silent except for the scribbling of the newswriters.

Constance moved through the formalities of confirming his identity and involvement in the incident as rapidly as she could, given his thick dialect.

"How many of you were in the group involved in the incident?"

"Eleven, Magistrate."

"And what had you been doing previously?"

"We been at pub."

"Drinking?"

"Yahs, Magistrate."

"Why did you have your tools with you?"

The man's mouth, which featured some truly hideous teeth — green and worn or missing — worked as he tried not to answer, but the geis compelled him.

"We was lookin' for shorties."

"Do you mean you were looking for dwarves?"

"Yahs."

"And what did you intend to do when you found them?"

Root muttered something.

"Speak clearly, Mister Root," said Constance sternly.

"We was gonna do 'em over."

"You were going to attack them?"

"Yahs." The man was sweating, trying not to answer.

"And did you attack the dwarf caravan in question when you found them?"

"Yaahs." Very reluctantly.

"In your statement given previously, you claimed that the dwarf caravan attacked you. Are you now saying that was untrue?"

"Yahs."

"You lied in your statement?"

"Yahs."

"Why did you lie, Mister Root?"

"Was sceered."

"You were scared. What were you scared of, Mister Root?"

"Sceered of Localgold." His answer was reluctant, and only just audible.

"And why was that?"

The man struggled visibly, but didn't answer.

"Are you under a compulsion not to answer that question, Mister Root?" she asked, knowing full well what the answer was.

"Yahs," he said, with a mixture of fear and relief.

"Did the Localgold suggest that you go out after the dwarves, Mister Root?"

Trustworthy popped up on his spring, but she waved him down. Root's eyes bulged as the conflicting geasa fought to force him in opposite directions.

"It's all right, Mister Root," Constance said after a few heartbeats, as the Copper's face started to flush, "you don't have to answer that question. Be it noted in the record that the witness was unable to answer.

"So you attacked the dwarf caravan. Another witness has told us that one of your group cried out, 'Get them!', or words to that effect. Did you hear those words, Mister Root?"

"Yahs."

"Who said them?"

"Sky Tanner." He added a tongue-click to the end of the name, as superstitious Coppers did to the names of the dead.

"And what happened then?"

"We run at the shorties and the horse-arse."

"Mister Root, in my courtroom you will call things by their correct names. You will call dwarves dwarves, gnomes gnomes, and centaurs centaurs. Is that clear?"

"Yahs, Magistrate."

"So what happened after Sky Tanner called out?"

"We run at the... the dwarves and the centaur."

"To attack them?"

"Yahs."

"With what object?"

"Magistrate?"

"What was your purpose? What did you hope to achieve by attacking them?"

"Beat 'em up, take their stuff."

"You were going to rob them?"

"Yahs," quietly.

"Did you intend to kill them?"

"Nah."

"Just to hurt them?"

"Yahs."

"And what stopped you?"

"The hor... the centaur."

"He stopped you from beating up the group any worse than you did, and from robbing them?"

"Yahs."

"What did he do to you?"

"Kicked me in guts." He touched the area in question and winced.

"Thank you, Mister Root. Yours to question," she said to Trustworthy.

Trustworthy waffled around for a while, trying to find an angle, but handed over to Hopeful without having elicited any further information — or obscured what had already come out. Hopeful tried to find out who had made the decision to attack the caravan, but Root still couldn't answer.

Constance dismissed Root, and brought out, one by one, the remaining eight Coppers. They added very little to Root's account, particularly since he had been on the scene and conscious later than any of them. None of them could answer the question of whose idea it was to attack the caravan. But they confirmed his testimony that their intent had been robbery and battery rather than murder.

"And how do you feel," asked Hopeful of one of the two who had been beating on the gnomes, "knowing that a gnome has died as a result of your actions?"

"Dunno," said the witness, whose name was Field.

"Does that bother you?"

"Dunno. Not much."

"Why is that then?"

"Just a gnome, weren't it?"

His companion, Hedge, said much the same.

Chapter 11: Verdict

"Call Pack of Sevenhills," said Constance. The dwarven section of the courtroom was becoming restive, and attempting to cast dark glances at the humans on the other side — an attempt mostly thwarted by the physical bulk of the guards, who stood facing in alternating directions with their shoulders overlapping.

The corporal fetched the dwarf, who was duly sworn.

"Mister Pack," said Constance, "you are the owner of the caravan that was attacked night before last near Boulder Bend?"

"Yes, Magistrate."

"So you are Mister Tree's employer of record?"

"Yes, Magistrate."

"And what was your relationship to the deceased gnome Pot?"

"He was my friend," said the dwarf quietly. A murmur ran through the room. Constance was aware that the local hold were mostly New Dwarves, meaning among other things that they were more relaxed than the traditional dwarves on the subject of gnome-dwarf relations. Even so, this was unusual.

"Your friend, Mister Pack?"

"Yes, Magistrate, my friend." The dwarf's head came up. He was comparatively young, his beard still brown, and its simple braids showed that he was a graduate in his craft, but not yet a master. "His family has... has belonged to mine for generations. We are... we were much the same age, and we grew up together. When I went on the road, he came with me, and he was my crew boss, my cook and my... my partner."

"He was your business partner?"

The dwarf hesitated for a moment, then said, "Yes, Magistrate."

"As of how long ago?"

"From the beginning. We shared the profits."

"But until recently you were not, legally, required..."

"Magistrate, it wasn't something we talked about publicly. It isn't usually done. And I'm from Sevenhills, it's not even in Denning, so the new law... Anyway, that was our arrangement. I know other dwarves will disapprove, but he was my friend and my partner and I miss him." There was more than a hint of tears in his large eyes, and, though it was of course impossible to see the set of his jaw through the beard, he managed to project determined defiance.

"I see," said Constance. She had a shrewd suspicion that the pair's partnership had not been simply an economic one, but she wasn't about to open that particular door in an already controversial case. She asked him, instead, about the profitability of his business and the contribution that Pot had made to it.

She led him through the incident briefly. He had nothing new to add, and said he couldn't identify the specific men who had bashed him and the gnomes — it had been dark, he had been frightened, and he found it hard to tell humans apart even in the daylight. There was some stirring and muttering among the humans at this, and Constance rang her bell.

The advocates had no questions for Pack, and agreed when Constance proposed that she not call the gnomes, since from their written statements they had not seen anything that Tree had not already reported.

She called the local healer, who had examined the men both living and dead, and confirmed the causes of death of the deceased Coppers.

Constance then handed the floor over to Trustworthy. The lawyer's task was to assemble the testimony into a coherent story that supported his side of the case and argue that the law should apply to his clients' benefit. He did his best, but the facts were against him, and Hopeful's brief response highlighted this quite clearly.

Constance gave the three peals on the bell that indicated that she was about to give judgement. She didn't feel the need to retire in order to consider.

"Bring out the prisoners," she instructed the corporal. "It is their right to hear the judgement given."

With the eight surviving Coppers, Pack and his five remaining gnomes, and especially Tree, plus the corporal and four guards, the platform was crowded, but they managed to squeeze in somehow. Constance rang the bell again for order.

"I will now make my determination regarding the deaths of Sky Tanner Pinegrove, Rock of the Hill Pinegrove, Moss Miller Pinegrove and Pot in Sevenhills.

"Regarding the death of Moss Miller Pinegrove, I find that he died having been kicked by a mule, which mule he had approached in order to steal it and/or its burden. Under the laws of Denning, this is a case of accidental death where the deceased's actions led to the accident, and furthermore occurred in attempted commission of an illegal act, and accordingly the owner of the mule in question, Mister Pack, is not liable."

The human side of the room stirred, but she glared them down.

"Regarding the deaths of Sky Tanner Pinegrove and Rock of the Hill Pinegrove, I find that they were killed by a duly licensed caravan guard in the course of attempted banditry, and accordingly..." the muttering had started when she said "banditry", and she stood and grasped her bell, but didn't ring it, "accordingly," she said more loudly, "their deaths place no liability on the caravan owner, Mister Pack." The guards facing the human side of the room unshipped their shouldered carbines and held them across their bodies, and the Coppers subsided, though they glared openly at the magistrate.

"Regarding the death of Pot in Sevenhills, I find that he was killed as an innocent bystander in the course of attempted banditry, and that all of those involved in the attempted banditry are liable for his death and the consequent economic loss to his employer, in addition to the missing mule. I hereby convict the following defendants, and their deceased collaborators, of attempted banditry and order that they or their heirs compensate Pack of Sevenhills to an amount to be independently assessed at another hearing. Be silent, or I will have you removed immediately from this court!" That was to the villagers, who were calling out angry words, despite the threats of the armed soldiers.

Constance began reading the names of the Coppers involved in the incident, over a rising tide of protest. The dark-grey-clad RBP men at the back of the hall rose, and the soldiers at the back began ordering them to sit down.

Constance broke off her listing of the Coppers and shouted, at the top of her voice, "Clear the court! Clear the court!" She couldn't be heard over the noise, even by the sergeant, who wasn't facing her but was watching the developing situation.

At that moment, one of the stained-glass windows near the platform shattered, and a dark, boxy object flew through it and bounced. It looked like an imagetaker, only smoking.

There was a frozen half-moment, then an unbelievably powerful tenor voice bellowed "Bomb!" next to Constance's ear, and large hands flipped her heavy judicial table and shoved her down behind it.

The explosion came almost simultaneously. The thick wooden tabletop thudded and splintered inward, and she was deafened completely. She only realized that the hands that had rescued her had been Tree's when she saw his hooves. He was still crouched over her protectively.

She could see, and also begin to hear faintly through the ringing in her ears, the sergeant bellowing orders. As she picked herself up and peeked over the table, she saw that several of the soldiers were smashing out more of the brickmakers' treasured window with the butts of their pressure carbines. They aimed the weapons through the window, and one of them called back to the sergeant something she couldn't make out.

"Stay down, please, Countygold," said Tree loudly in her ear. "You all right, Mister Pack?"

The dwarf and his gnomes were also crouched behind the table, and Tree. In turning to look at them, Constance's gaze swept across the Coppers whom she had just convicted of banditry. One of them was down, bleeding from a gash in his head that hadn't been there before. Screaming faded in as her hearing recovered.

"Thank you, Mister Tree," she said, once Pack and the gnomes had reported themselves unhurt and she had settled her back against the underside of the still-tipped table. "That was quick thinking."

The centaur nodded, once, his eyes sweeping the chaos. The two guards that had been on the members of the caravan had been called off to other duties, but the two on the Coppers were still there and still alertly guarding their charges. One had a torn sleeve, but appeared uninjured.

The healer who had testified earlier crossed into her field of vision and checked the man who was down. He spoke inaudibly to one of the man's friends, who pressed a rag to the head wound in response, and hurried off.

"What's the situation?" asked Constance, who was accustomed to being informed.

"Looks like one or two dead from the bomb, several others wounded," said Tree, his eyes darting back and forth across what she could only imagine was a scene of chaos.

"Shouldn't we be getting out of here?" she asked.

"We're in a structure with thick walls, and our attackers aren't. We control the approaches now. It would be a bad strategic move to exit at the moment."

Her hearing was largely back now, and the screaming was diminishing as the sergeant and his soldiers got the situation under control.

"They've contained the RBP at the back — got them down on the floor, a few casualties..."

"What? What happened?"

"They tried to take advantage of the confusion, but these troops are good."

The chaos was dying down enough that Constance said, "Get me my bell."

"Countygold?"

"Get me my bell. I'll quiet them down. It's tied into the court mindspell."

Tree made a concise gesture to one of the gnomes, who circled the upended table and handed Constance's bell to her. She thanked him, stood up, and rang it authoritatively.

"Silence!" she called. "Silence!"

The noise died back to the occasional groan from one of the wounded. Now that she was standing, she could see the extent of the devastation — less than she had feared, but more than she had hoped. Her table was set near the front of the platform, back a little from the edge so that there was room for a witness to stand where she could see them without cricking her neck. Pack and the gnomes, warned by Tree's shout and used to following his lead, had dived behind it when Tree had flipped it, and appeared uninjured.

The newswriters, behind their long table on the dwarf side of the room, had not escaped unharmed. One of them clutched a rag to his bleeding head, and looked about to faint. The healer ministered to another, binding up his shoulder. A third had been laid on the desk, unconscious or possibly dead.

The dwarves seated behind the newswriters had only a couple of minor injuries. They had probably ducked behind the high seat backs of the people in front of them.

At the lawyers' bench, on the other side, Hopeful was white-faced with shock, apart from where he was spattered with blood, and was putting pressure on his left shoulder. Trustworthy lay face-down across the table in a pool of blood which appeared to be originating from his chest. It was oozing, not pumping, and she guessed that he was dead. By his position, he had been standing to protest the verdict when the bomb came through the window.

A few others on the humans' side of the room were also injured, apart from the defendant whom she had noticed earlier. One woman had a long cut across her cheek, which bled copiously, as cuts to the face do.

At the back of the room were several sprawled bodies in dark grey, and one man in the black of the Realm troops sat propped against a bench. She couldn't see what injuries he had. The little pressure carbines fired quietly, and she hadn't heard them through her deafness and the earlier noise, but it was clear that the soldiers had fought off an attempted attack by the RBP. The rest of the RBP men were on their knees, hands behind their heads, under the guns of five soldiers.

Like most Denningers of her age and class, Constance had served in the military in her youth. As a High Gold, she had, of course, been an officer, and one of the first things she had learned was what she privately thought of as the Sergeant Ritual. Invoking it, she thought, would reassure everyone, probably including the sergeant. She spoke the opening words in her best officer voice: "Sergeant, report."

The sergeant saluted her out of reflex, stood to attention and barked:

"Countygold! We have come under attack from a person as yet unidentified who introduced an explosive device through the window here." He indicated the broken panes, through which two soldiers were now peering. "The person concerned appears to have absconded following the attack and prior to our securing of the window concerned. In the subsequent confusion the... persons at the back of the room attempted to seize weapons from my men and were repulsed."

Constance had, of course, worked all of this out for herself, but having the sergeant say it was part of the ritual. She completed it with the words all good junior officers learn early and use often.

"Very good, Sergeant," she said, "carry on."

The sergeant saluted again and shouted a couple more orders, including asking for a report from the soldier stationed outside the door on the side where the attack had been made.

"Didn't see it, Sarge," came the reply through the heavy door. "There's a big pillar thing what blocks the view. By the time I got around it he'd scarpered. Wait," she continued, as the soldiers looking out the window also tensed.

"Sarge," one of them said, "the imagetakers are coming with a prisoner."

The sergeant, who was short, had to stand on a protruding ridge of brick at the base of the wall to see out of the window. "Pass the prisoner and the ones holding him in," he ordered the soldier outside.

The soldier inside the door opened it in response to a prearranged coded knock from the outside guard, and two of the imagetakers hauled what Constance recognized as a third of their number through the doorway.

"We caught this chap making an escape," said one of them. "We think he's your bomber."

"That's my imagetaker!" protested one of the newswriters.

"Who are you?" demanded the sergeant, turning to the newswriter who had spoken.

"Boldness Newswriter, *Realm Benefit*."

This news received frowns from the sergeant, Constance and a number of others. The bomb had been in the form of an imagemaker, all right, and for it to have been thrown by the imagetaker from the RBP's newspaper made all too much sense.

"Swear him in," said Constance decisively. "This is a courtroom, temporary or not, and the spells are good. Swear him in and ask him if he threw the bomb. Mister Hopeful, will you act for him?" The law, and the spells, required a lawyer to be present and acting for the accused at an arraignment. Hopeful nodded bravely, still clutching his bleeding shoulder.

Facing the evidence of his act — especially the corpse of Trustworthy — the imagetaker's defiance wilted enough that the court officials were able to swear him in. As expected, he was unable to deny that he had thrown the bomb, though he did not admit it, remaining stubbornly silent. Inability to deny a crime under geis being sufficient evidence to bring a charge, the imagetaker was bound over for trial. The same treatment was given, by virtue of known association, to the newswriter, though she, under geis, denied knowledge of the bomb.

Because the attack had been, in part, against the Countygold, she couldn't try the case. It had to go to her Provincegold, Tenacious Northriver. As the attempt of the RBP men to seize the guards' weapons was clearly part of the same attack, those of them who had survived the tussle were included in the same case. The soldiers marched them, and the convicted bandits, out to the town lockup, which they crowded severely, and then let the dwarves, gnomes and humans of the audience disperse.

Under Tree's direction, the dwarves and gnomes formed up into a defensive column, most senior on the inside, and marched away. He turned back for a moment and gave the Countygold the traditional military salute of an open hand over the heart, which she returned. He was old enough, she thought, that he might have fought on the other side during the trade "disputes" with Coriant, back when she was an officer. Their centaur troops had been formidable, and had been a large part of the reason that the issue had been settled more to Coriant's satisfaction than Denning's.

Chapter 12: City Guard

When Constance returned to her manor, she contacted Determined on the farspeaker and reported the outcome of the trial, including the tragic aftermath.

"Well done," he said. "That was a brave verdict to give."

She snorted. "It was the clearest case of banditry I've ever seen. I'm not going to give the wrong verdict in a trial in case it upsets some ranting little upstart."

"Nevertheless, it will upset him, and his supporters, and I want you protected. How defensible is your home?"

"It's a manor, not a castle. We're far enough from the border that my ancestors felt safe building something without arrow slits in it. It will hold off a peasant mob, though, and has."

"Will it hold off armed troops?" he asked.

"No," she said reluctantly.

"It might be a good idea for you to come to the capital. Just until things quiet down."

"I'm the Countygold. I can't just..."

"Constance," he said, "they are quite capable of torching your home with you in it."

"Realmgold," she said, "let them try it."

He sighed.

"I can't send you any more troops, you know," he said. "I need them all. Truth be told, I need the ones you have already."

Constance considered. Defiance was one thing, but without more troops her manor really was indefensible. And yet, her garden... She didn't want to leave it for long, it would run wild.

"Well, if you need the troops back, perhaps I could come with them to the capital for a few days. But I hate running from that hateful little ranter."

"You're running towards him, actually. His county is right next to the city. Tell you what, I'll announce that I'm preparing guidelines for similar trials and need you to consult. It can even be the truth."

"Very well," she said reluctantly. "When and how?"

"I'll send a skyboat," he said. "Overland travel is too risky. Half the counties between you and here are overrun with RBP supporters."

"All right," she said. "I'll warn the sergeant."

The skyboat was a sleek craft, like a fast water-borne boat with a transparent canopy over the top and stubby wings for maneuvering (the actual flight, she understood, was achieved through some sort of dwarven crystal technology). Constance had never flown before, skyboats being a new and expensive phenomenon, and found the sensation vexatious. She endured the noise, the vibration, the hard seats, and the closeness of rather sweaty troops with Gold stoicism.

When they disembarked, she was surprised to find that the Realmgold himself had come out to meet her. She bowed to the appropriate degree, he bowed in reply to the appropriate lesser degree, and they walked side-by-side into the palace, surrounded by their joint troops.

"Your majordomo reports that there is a small crowd outside the gates," he told her. "So far, no attempts to scale the wall."

"There are spikes on top," she said. "I hope they try it."

He smiled, and led her inside.

That evening, he described Constance's verdict to Victory. She considered carefully, and then said, in her quiet, unemphatic way, "I believe I like the Countygold of Blueclay."

"I'm fond of her myself," he said.

"How old is she?" she asked, surprising him.

"Oh, around fifty," he said.

"Good," she said, obscurely. "So what has been the reaction to the judgement?"

"Predictable. According to the pro-RBP papers, the whole affair was a massive miscarriage of justice. They had to distort the few facts they gave quite severely, and separate them with large tracts of opinion, to achieve that effect, of course. According to *Realm Benefit* itself, troops acting under my orders attacked a peaceful protest against the verdict — they imply it was outside the courtroom — and several protesters and the lawyer for their side were killed in the fracas and a number of others, including their own imagetaker, wrongly imprisoned."

"Speaking of which, what have you done with them?"

"What I had to. Sent them to the Provincegold's court,

charged with attacking the court of a countygold. Unfortunately, the Provincegold of Northriver is practically an open RBP supporter, and if he doesn't dismiss the charges I'll be very surprised."

"What do the other papers say?"

"They report the verdict fairly and straightforwardly, give or take their own taste for sensationalism."

"Good. And public reaction?"

He sobered. "There have been stones thrown through the windows of dwarf businesses, RBP slogans daubed on their walls. Nothing worse so far."

"Prepare for it," she advised.

Determined sighed over his morning newspaper. He wished Victory had been wrong just this once.

A large dwarf building — one of the ones that was factory, warehouse, shop and living quarters combined — had been set on fire, with a number of dwarves and gnomes inside. At least ten had perished.

Worse than that, witnesses reported that a unit of the city guard had stood by and done nothing to arrest those responsible.

"Reliable!" he called. His secretary, alerted by the tone of his voice, hurried in.

"I want to see the commander of the city guard. Immediately."

"Yes, Realmgold."

The commander was barely respectful enough to keep from being arrested. He disclaimed all knowledge of any such incident, with a smirk that implied, "You know I'm lying but there's nothing you can do about it."

Trained in mindmagic up to the rank of a mage-minor, Determined could, indeed, tell that he was lying, though probably so could a half-witted farmhand. Here, clearly, was a man who believed that the Realmgold had so little power that a minor official could defy him with impunity.

"Who do you report to?" he asked the smirking commander.

"The Countygold of Lakeside Koslin," he said, omitting the respectful "Realmgold".

"Reliable," called Determined. When the secretary appeared, he said, "The commander will await my convenience in the small waiting room while you get the Countygold of Lakeside Koslin in here."

The commander looked slightly worried at this, but only slightly.

It took an hour and a half to locate the Countygold and bring her in, protesting mildly at the disruption to her day. Reliable settled her in front of the Realmgold's desk and disappeared again to fetch the commander, only to come back without him.

"Uh, Realmgold, the commander has left."

"Left?"

"Yes, Realmgold. He's not in the waiting room and the guards on the door say he left."

Determined opened his mouth, then closed it again. The guards, of course, were not aware of his order that the commander should wait. But the commander certainly was.

"Have him arrested," he said.

"Realmgold?" asked the Countygold.

"I told him very distinctly to wait here until you arrived. He was already being insolent and obstructive. I want him relieved of command and arrested."

"With respect, Realmgold, I believe that's my decision," the Countygold said, drawing herself up.

Determined glared at her. "It is, indeed, your decision whether he is relieved of command, though I hope you will place weight on the wishes of your Realmgold," he said, with the precise diction of a man trying not to lose his temper. "However, I *can* have him arrested. See to it," he said to Reliable, who shifted and cleared his throat.

"Ah, Realmgold, to whom should I convey that command? You see, normally I would send it to, uh…"

"The commander of the city guard, yes. Send my guard."

"The Salvanusmouth mercenaries?"

"Yes."

"Yes, Realmgold."

Determined's polite instinct was to apologize to the Countygold, but he quashed it sternly. Then he reconsidered. He needed her goodwill.

"My apologies for your unnecessary trip, Countygold. When I tell a subordinate to stay in a room I do not anticipate that he will take it upon himself to leave. I will give you more notice in future if I can."

After a significant moment, the Countygold thanked him and gave a precisely judged bow, which he returned.

When the clicking of her hard shoes on the marble floors had receded beyond hearing, Determined called Reliable in again and had him summon the Head Intelligencer.

"Here's my problem," he said, when the man had

reported. "At least the City Guard and probably the Army are rife with RBP sympathizers. I can't maintain civil order under those conditions. I want the disloyal elements purged, and to do that I need to know who they are."

The intelligencer looked grave. "That isn't going to be easy, Realmgold. Even if we can establish loyalty, there'll be resistance."

"Establish loyalty. Good idea. We can give them a loyalty test. Reliable!"

Reliable appeared at the door.

"Draft an announcement. All people bearing arms in the service of Denning, including militia and regular military, will report to the nearest magistrate within four days, no, two days, and they will take a binding loyalty vow specifically stating that they will act to keep the peace in defense of dwarves, gnomes and any other speaking beings just as they would for humans. They will, furthermore, not accept orders which originate from anyone other than the legitimate government of the Realm of Denning."

"Realmgold, we can't impose that on the private forces of the various Golds, and the City Guard belong to the Countygold, not the Realm," the intelligencer said over Reliable's frantic scribbling.

"That's true, we can't. I'll have to ask... That is, I'll take advice on that point and get back to you. But let's begin with the Realm's forces, at least." The standard military vow was simply to follow the orders of one's superiors and the military regulations, which left, in his view, far too much room for interpretation in the absence of specific instructions.

Another hour and a half passed without incident, and

then Reliable brought in a winded messenger in the uniform of the Salvanusmouth mercenary rifles.

"Realmgold," he gasped, "City Guard have forted up in their HQ and refuse to surrender their commander."

"Can you keep them contained?"

"Only if they don't get reinforced from other stations. And they may do. They go lightly armed for the most part, but the stations contain bows and spears and riot gear. The HQ is well-built for defense, too."

Determined muttered a curse.

"Pull back to surrounding buildings and keep them bottled up if you can. Reliable, you sent out that announcement of the loyalty vow?"

"I did, Realmgold."

"Find out if we have a unit who have taken it already and send them to relieve my guard."

"Are you declaring martial law, Realmgold?"

The messenger, his breath now easing, watched the Realmgold for his answer just as eagerly as did the secretary.

"Not yet. But as soon as I have enough sworn forces, I am relieving the City Guard of responsibility for civil order within Lakeside Koslin."

As Reliable vanished to the outer office again, Determined called after him, "And have someone fetch the Countygold of Blueclay. I need to talk to her."

Constance, when Determined had briefed her, looked grave.

"You're risking civil war, you realize," she said.

"I do. But I think we're headed in that direction anyway. Better to force the issue, make people take a stand early so we're prepared if it all falls apart."

"I can't disagree. But speaking of taking a stand, have you asked your supporters to swear their people to the same vow?"

"No — good thinking. Reliable!"

The word went out over the farspeaker, along with the announcement of a speech he would give the following day. He would speak in the plaza in front of the library, but he would have a farspeaker with him and his supporters throughout the realm would be able to hear it. He only wished there were more of them.

He and Constance drafted it together all that afternoon, occasionally interrupted by reports.

"The Countygold of Lakeside Koslin has openly declared allegiance to the RBP."

"Not a surprise. Do we still have the city guard bottled up?"

"Yes. A few stations have surrendered and we've disarmed them, which is useful, because we need their cells to hold rioters."

"Good. Offer the others inducements to surrender as well. Amnesty if they do, assault of their station if they don't. Water in front and fire behind."

"Yes, Realmgold."

"Rioting and looting in the crafter district. Human businesses as well as dwarf ones."

"Do you have it contained?"

"Yes, but we're short of places to put the rioters."

"Any more guard stations surrendered?"

"A few. A lot are holding out, though."

"Don't we have dungeons here?"

"Realmgold, they haven't been used for a century."

"They'll be good and dank, then. Open them up, make sure they're secure and take the rioters down there. Any city guard you arrest, too."

"Yes, Realmgold."

"And Lieutenant, what's that rag on your arm?" It was held on with a common cheap military arm-ring, dented copper, which he could feel was a token bound into the loyalty vow. Anyone else who had taken the vow, if they had enough mindmagic to be a sergeant, would be able to tell from three or four paces away that the man was sworn to the same cause.

"Loyalist brassard, Realmgold. Everyone who's taken the oath has one, so you can tell who's who from a distance. Since we have so many different uniforms."

"Why dark green?"

"Your jacket, Realmgold."

Determined glanced down. He was wearing his favorite jacket, which was, indeed, dark green. He hadn't realized it was so characteristic.

"Ah, thank you, Lieutenant, carry on."

"Realmgold, I've compiled a list of High Golds and their declared allegiances. Thought you might want…"

"Yes, thank you, Reliable, good initiative."

"Numbers at the bottom, Realmgold."

"Ah. Not so good."

Denning was a large realm. It had more than 90 counties in its six provinces, and of these, 16 Countygolds and one

Provincegold (Beauty Six Gorges) had declared for Determined. That they knew of, nine Countygolds had declared for Silverstones and the RBP, but the information was incomplete and there were another 12 listed as "probable".

And the Provincegold of Northriver was a "probable" for Silverstones as well.

"So much for those thugs who attacked your courtroom coming to trial," remarked Determined, tapping the line. "He'll probably just let them go quietly."

"I never liked him," said Constance.

"Me either. Well, let's finish up this speech. There's someone I want to show it to tonight."

Chapter 13: Writs of Attainder

Just before the normal appointed time for his conversation with Victory, Determined swore Constance to secrecy and then took her to the room where he had the farviewer set up.

"Where did you get these magic mirrors and farspeakers?" she asked, as he touched the crystal that started it up. He pronounced the activating word, and the image began to form, slowly as it always did.

"Koskant," he said, in answer to her question.

"You're in communication with Koskant?"

"Not just with Koskant. Watch."

"Good evening, Determined," said Victory as the image cleared and stabilized. "Is that the Countygold of Blueclay with you?" She had her glamour up, having presumably noticed as the image formed on her end that Determined was not alone.

"Yes, I hope you don't mind. I've taken her oath of secrecy."

"Of course, if you trust her that is good enough for me. Good evening, Countygold, I have heard excellent things of you."

Constance was looking back and forth between Determined and the image of Victory, as disconcerted as he had yet seen her. "Ah, good evening... Realmgold Victory?" she guessed. Victory nodded in her regal manner.

"I hear rumors of rioting," she said.

Victory, of course, would have agents in place with farspeakers, and the "rumors" would be considerably more than that. Allies or not, each realm spied on the other in order to keep in practice. Determined, politely pretending that this wasn't the case, summarized the day's events quickly.

"So I've scheduled a speech for tomorrow morning," he concluded. "We've been working on it all afternoon."

"I would like to hear it," she said.

As usual, Victory made a few well-judged suggestions, more to do with the manner of the speech than the content.

"So in general, you think it a good speech?" asked Determined.

"I think it an excellent speech. I think it will precipitate confrontation, of course. But better now than when the RBP have had more time to build up their forces."

"My thought, also," said Constance, who had become increasingly comfortable with Victory as their discussion of the speech progressed.

"I'm very much afraid," said Determined, "that I'm leading my country into civil war."

"Better than not leading it," said Constance.

"The Countygold is correct," said Victory. "Civil war is coming anyway. By taking a stand, you make it less likely that the RBP and their narrow views will prevail."

Determined scowled, but nodded reluctantly.

"May I make a suggestion?" she continued.

"Always."

"Brief your intelligencers and your loyal commanders. Tell them what to do if, for any reason, you are not in a position to direct them. Develop a plan now in case you need it tomorrow."

Constance's eyes went wide, but Determined nodded.

"I'd already planned to," he said.

The briefings took all night. Skycouriers, messengers, military officers and intelligencers came and went constantly. By morning, Determined was red-eyed, pale and exhausted, but as confident as he could be that everything was in place.

Surrounded by Salvanusmouth mercenaries, trailed by Constance on his right and Reliable on his left, he marched down to the plaza.

It was early, and the plaza was cold in the wind blowing off the Inland Sea, but there was a slowly growing crowd. The newswriters were at the front with their imagetakers. Loyalist troops ringed the space in a half-oval extending from the front of the library, wearing the dark-green armbands that showed they had taken the vow. Anyone wearing dark grey was politely but firmly excluded from the circle. Of course, thought Determined, for some this only meant that they would leave the plaza, remove their dark-grey armband or coat, re-enter from another direction and be passed through, but it was something. And at least if they took the coats off they'd freeze.

He stepped up to the podium, carrying his notes, and Reliable handed him two folders.

"Citizens of Denning," he began, and then waited for the crowd to quiet.

"Citizens of Denning, you will have heard that I have begun to take vows from my loyal troops to defend all the people of Denning, regardless of their background. You will have heard, also, that I have instructed my troops to take over the preservation of public order in the city, because the city guard were failing in their duty. Failing to protect human homes and businesses, as well, I would note. Fire does not care who owns a building. It will spread to wherever it can burn. And, as you will know if you read the papers which report all the facts, human businesses have been looted and damaged in the riots which were supposedly against dwarves and gnomes.

"And this is what I am here to tell you this morning. Some are attempting to portray our current struggle as being over the issue of who is a Denninger, of who is entitled to the protection of the law, of who is worthy to be considered a citizen. My answer is that a worthy citizen is someone who contributes to the wellbeing of Denning, to its productivity, not to its destruction. And this is true regardless of the language that citizen speaks, regardless of the shape of that citizen's body, the number of their fingers, or the color of their hair. It is with the actions of citizens that I am concerned, whether they build up Denning or tear it down, whether they give or only take.

"For the greater issue, my fellow citizens, my fellow Denningers, is order and the rule of law. The greater issue is, how is Denning to be ruled: by law and legitimate succession, for the benefit of all, or by anyone who can whip a mob into a frenzy?

"That issue concerns each one of us. And each one of us must answer that question.

"In particular, those who are the established preservers of law and order, tradition and governance, must answer that question. So I have here in my hands two sets of papers.

"In my right hand," he said, raising it, "are writs of commission, some of which I have already signed. They bear the names of each Countygold and Provincegold in Denning, and they promise that each High Gold who takes the loyalty vow, and gives it to their troops as I have given it to mine, may join those troops to mine and have them considered as troops of the realm. What is more, each such High Gold will be considered an officer of the realm, to be defended by the troops of the realm, wheresoever those troops come from."

He paused to allow the audience to think through the implications, then he dropped the folder to the lectern with a thump.

"In my left hand," he said, raising it in turn, "are a smaller number of writs of attainder, which I have not signed. These are in the names of each Countygold and Provincegold who has not yet offered their support to me. Should any such High Gold give vow or oath to a force or group opposing the forces of the realm, or commit their personal troops against the troops of the realm, I will consider that an act of rebellion, the act of a traitor who is not worthy to hold High Gold rank. I shall then declare that High Gold attainted from their rank, and appoint another in their place. The Countygold of Lakeside Koslin's writ is on the top. I am giving her until noon tomorrow to return to her allegiance to the Realm, command her troops to surrender and both take the vow of loyalty herself and administer it to her forces. Otherwise, with regret, I will declare her tenure of the County void by cause of treason and appoint another as Countygold. If her family disclaim her as their head and swear loyalty, I am prepared to consider another whom they appoint. Otherwise, that family will lose their ancient post and I will give it to a deserving candidate who is loyal to the Realm and will protect *all* the citizens of this County.

"I am a man of peace, as you all know. But I am not a meek man. I will not allow my realm, our realm, the realm we love, to be torn apart by an illegitimate desire for power or by a greedy, angry rabble or by words of hatred and disunity.

"I do not want war. I do not want brother against brother, Denninger against Denninger. But I will not hold back from whatever needs to be done to keep Denning free, and just, and whole, and *ruled by law*.

"So to the High Golds, I say this. Send to me your sworn and bound and witnessed vow that you, and any troops you have, have taken the vow of loyalty, and I will return to you my commission." He lifted the folder in his right hand. "You will enjoy all the benefits of joining with me and with others who want to keep our realm peaceful and well-ordered.

"And to the Localgolds, I say the same. I hope I will not need any new Countygolds. But if I do, it is to Localgolds who have shown their loyalty that I will turn first.

"And to the ordinary Denninger, I say: Consider the actions and the loyalty of your Golds. Consider your own conscience. If you want to be a part of a united, peaceful Denning ruled by law, if you want to be part of preserving such a realm, go to any loyal magistrate and take the vow of loyalty, and then to any existing force that has taken the vow — which you may identify by their color of dark green — and I will be glad to have you. Together let us make a better future for ourselves and for each other in Denning.

"Join me, all of you, for in unity we will find our strength."

He took one step down and stood by the lectern, as a signal that he had finished. Applause broke out in the crowd, and he smiled and waved. A movement high up in one of the buildings surrounding the plaza caught his eye, and he turned his head, only to have a burly guard leap in front of him and another shove him to the ground.

The pop of the pressure gun was inaudible over the applause. The guard in front jerked and grunted, falling partly on top of Determined, and others took his place and began to return fire. As they did so, a mass of grey-clad men rushed the outer circle of guards just as they were turning outwards, and simultaneously, members of the crowd attacked the guards from behind at the same point, breaking the line.

"Go, go, go!" shouted the guard sergeant. "Get the Realmgold to safety. Into the library, Route K, go, go!"

Determined cursed to himself as he fumbled his personal shield on. After a night without sleep, focussed on his speech, he had forgotten it. Two of his guards carried their fallen comrade between them. He was alive, but bleeding heavily from his meaty upper arm, and muttering steadily in Tenus, his native language. Determined knew diplomatic Tenus, but these words were new to him. He assumed they were not diplomatic.

The library wasn't yet open, but they had a passkey. Locking the doors behind them, they hustled Determined,

Constance, Reliable — whose eyes were as big and white as a pair of dinner plates — and the wounded man past the tall stacks and into the administrative area at the back, which had stairs to the roof.

"Shut up, Black!" said one of the bearers to the wounded soldier, who was still cursing steadily.

"It helps with the pain," said the man through clenched teeth.

"Don't be such a child. Come on, get him up those stairs."

One of the unit's corporals was working the farspeaker. "No fire received as yet by the transport," he reported.

"Good, let's hurry and maybe there won't be any," said the sergeant. "Come on, Mister Secretary, keep up!" Reliable started, and picked up his pace. He was panting on the steep stairs.

"If we're going to be doing this, we need to get you into training," said Constance, who was showing no signs of being winded despite being twice Reliable's age.

Just then, a loud smashing sound came from behind and below them, back where the library doors were. Reliable's eyes grew, if anything, wider, and he found some extra speed he hadn't known he had.

They burst out on the roof beside the door of a skyboat, one of Victory's sleek Gryphon-class boats, with room for eight people besides the pilot. Determined, Constance, Reliable, the wounded man and his two helpers piled in, and the sergeant and the remaining five troops prepared to defend the door to the stairs. The sergeant slammed the hatch and called to the pilot, "Go! Ware fire from the rooftops!"

The skyboat shot up like a cork that had been held at the

bottom of a basin and turned for the nearby palace. Reliable went even paler, and retched, but managed to contain his breakfast by a heroic effort.

"Thank you," said Determined, turning to the soldier who had taken the bullet for him.

"Don't mention it, Realmgold," said the man, still through gritted teeth.

"Oh, but I do. It was a brave action, and I shan't forget it."

"It'll all be on your bill, Realmgold," said one of the other guards, half-jokingly. Like most rulers' personal guards, the troops were mercenary riflemen from the city-state of Salvanusmouth.

"I look forward to it. Thank you all."

By this point, the skyboat had started to descend again into the courtyard of the palace. It landed neatly and the group piled out, slightly less precipitately than they had climbed in, and stood blinking on the stones while the skyboat took on a gunner and his swivel-mounted heavy weapon and flew back to assist with the situation in the plaza.

"Well," said Determined, "I'm definitely getting better at public speaking. Though that's really more of a response than I was looking for."

Nobody laughed, but Constance smiled a rather grim smile.

"As long as we get the response we want from the Golds," she said.

Later that evening, Determined received his guard captain's report.

"We have ten of our people injured," he said. "None

killed, but there were at least six civilians killed in the riot, and several badly burned."

"Burned?"

"Yes, the library was set on fire."

Determined winced. "Much damage?"

"Mostly to the front rooms."

Determined felt guilty at his relief that the ancient book collection, at the back of the building, had been spared. Six people were dead, he reminded himself.

"Several of the injured among the civilians were newswriters," continued the captain. "Their papers have covered the riot extensively. Oh, and the Countygold of Lakeside Koslin has repeated her declaration for the RBP and encouraged her troops to oppose us. She's forted up in her manor and won't come out."

Determined sighed, and pulled the folder of writs of attainder towards him. He took out the uppermost sheet of paper and signed it.

"Give that to my secretary on the way out, please," he said. "And tell him to send a copy to the papers."

Chapter 14: Reliable's Oath

Sometime in the evening — Determined had lost track of the time — Reliable tapped hesitantly at his door and carried in a tray of food.

"Is it dinnertime?"

"Yes, Realmgold. A little after, if anything."

"Thanks, Reliable. I don't know what I'd do without you."

Reliable cast his eyes down and bit his lip, then carried the tray over to the desk and set it down. The food was simple, flatbread wrapped around meat and vegetables, the kind of meal that could be eaten while working without too much risk of soiling papers.

"Have you eaten?" Determined asked the secretary.

"Not yet."

"Join us, then." There was enough on the tray for three, especially since Constance seemed to eat very little. "Draw up a chair."

"Thank you, Realmgold."

There was silence while they addressed themselves to the food, and then Reliable cleared his throat.

"Uh, Realmgold, there's something I want to talk to you about."

Determined, his mouth full, gave a "Go on" gesture with the hand that was less occupied with holding his food.

"I'd like to swear a loyalty oath. To you directly."

Determined swallowed. "You know, Reliable, I had never given a thought to whether you were loyal. You've always lived up to your name, and..."

"Thank you, Realmgold. But it's not that. It's..." he looked down at the depopulated tray that sat between them. "I'm not a brave man," he said. "Never have been. But you are, and I'd like to bind myself to you. In... in the hope that some of it may transfer."

Determined, for a moment, didn't know what to think.

"Nobody has ever called me brave before," he said. "Thank you."

"It's true," put in Constance. "You are."

"Well," he said, "thank you both. One witness is held sufficient for an oath between master and servant, if I remember correctly?"

"That's right," said Constance, "and it would be my pleasure."

"Well then," said Determined. "Let's do it. I assume, Reliable, that with your usual efficiency you've prepared a form of words?"

Reliable smiled, just a little. "Yes, Realmgold." He hurried out to his own office and returned with a scroll-case. "This is based on the historic oath between Realmgold Might and her faithful maid Waterspring. With appropriate changes," he said, unrolling the triplicate oathforms.

Determined recognized the work of the palace's Office of

Oaths, Vows and Geasa. The forms were beautiful, featuring interlaced geometric sigils with flowers and leaves peeping through the gaps, accented with gold ink. Across the three-part magical diagram were the words of the ritual, his in one part, Reliable's in another and Constance's in the third, written in Reliable's best calligraphy using the formal Elvish alphabet. In the centre was a circle where they would seal, sign and thumbprint to witness the oath.

Determined scanned the paper and nodded. "All right, come round this side and we'll begin."

As was proper for such an oath, Reliable knelt and put his hands between those of Determined. Constance held the oathform so that all three could read from it. Although, as the head of a Gold family, she was automatically a priest in the Asterist religion, as well as a magistrate, neither priest nor magistrate was mandatory for an oath of loyalty. She would merely be a witness, though an especially well-qualified one, and as such she had no lines until the end.

"Are there tokens?" she asked, glancing down the paper. "They aren't obligatory, of course, but they are usual."

"Oh!" said Reliable, and, taking one hand from Determined's light clasp, fished in his pocket. "I obtained these, Realmgold. I hope you approve." He held out his palm, on which were a matched pair of service oathrings, opals mounted in silver. They were men's rings, bulky, ornamented with scrollwork in a slightly old-fashioned style, and clearly second-hand, though in good condition.

"Those are excellent," said Determined. "How much for my one?"

"A quarter hammer," replied the secretary. Part of the rite was that each person paid for one token and gave it to the other, which was why oathrings for service tended to be relatively inexpensive. Determined nodded, and Reliable, taking back both of his hands, placed the rings in the circle at the centre of the form, where they could be reached at the appropriate point. Then he took the Realmgold's purse from his left pocket, extracted four copper anvils, and transferred the square, dwarf-minted coins to his own purse in his right pocket.

They resumed their positions and began. Reliable, as the junior partner in the oath, spoke first.

"My Gold, my Realmgold and my master, I offer to you my loyalty, fealty and submission by oath of my heart, mind and body, to serve you always faithfully for the high regard that is between us two. And so I call this witness here present to attest, affirm and testify."

Determined answered, "My subject, my secretary and my servant, I accept from you your loyalty, fealty and submission, to which I give high value, honor and praise. I offer you my support, protection and patronage by oath of my heart, mind and body, to requite your faithful service always with honor for the high regard that is between us two. And so I call this witness here present to attest, affirm and testify." He squeezed Reliable's hands momentarily and released them.

"Honored Gold," said Reliable, taking up one of the rings, "I accept your support, protection and patronage, and offer you this token of the bond between us, that it, too, may be a witness always present of the oath we have made." He handed the ring over, and Determined slipped it on the forefinger of his right hand, the hand of alliance and allegiance.

"Honored Secretary," he said, taking the other ring, "I

offer you this token of the bond between us, that it, too, may be a witness always present of the oath we have made." He gave it to Reliable, who slid it onto his finger. They turned to Constance, who, holding the paper at a distance to help her eyesight, read from it: "In my presence this oath is concluded, and I attest, affirm and testify that it is a good and true oath."

As she spoke the words, both men felt the oath take firm hold. Determined nodded at his secretary, and the little man smiled nervously back.

"Do you know," said Constance, after they had signed, sealed and thumbprinted the three copies and taken one each, "I believe I would like to make a personal oath to you myself. Not just the general loyalty vow to the realm."

"Thank you, Constance. Tonight?"

"Not tonight. I will sit with your good secretary and put something together. It ought to be done publicly, I think."

"I appreciate that greatly," said Determined, "more than I can say. From both of you. I… have not experienced much personal loyalty before."

"You're maturing," said Constance. "There's more to be loyal to."

"I hope so," he said.

Chapter 15: Treaty Issues

In Gulfport, the cloaked man visited his Gold ally again, and "spontaneous" riots broke out in sympathy for those taking place in Denning. Dwarf shops were vandalized, a few badly-spelled Human Purity slogans were painted on buildings, and several free gnomes were set upon and assaulted.

Victory immediately scheduled a speech in Magnificence Plaza, the Gulfport equivalent of the library steps. It was packed with people, including many gnomes and a few dwarves.

"You have heard," she said, "of the trouble in the north, where our good neighbor Denning is split between supporters of the Realmgold and his rule of law and a rabble of troublemakers and traitors. Those traitors — for so he names them, and I agree — claim validation from misguided ideas of 'human purity', and yet their actions harm humans just as much as anyone else. The same is the case here, where criminals have been hired to riot in support of the Denninger rebels, and have harmed honest businesses and the homes of good people and have assaulted our citizens.

"That is not our way as a people. We have lived at peace with our neighbors within the Realm since before the memory of the oldest person here. And no rented rioters are going to change that." Victory always spoke calmly and without raising her voice, and this speech was no exception, but she put a grim tone and a clear emphasis into that sentence.

"So I call upon the people of Koskant to unite in support of the rule of law. I am calling up the militias, and I am giving them the task of protecting their own neighborhoods and their own neighbors, whether human, dwarf or gnome. My regular troops will support you in this endeavor, because *I will not have* this rioting and destruction."

Over the next few days, the dwarves, who had started to regard Victory as their enemy after her emancipation of the gnomes, were placed in the confusing position of being defended by her troops and the neighborhood militias. A number of attempted attacks fizzled out in the face of the men and women, armed mostly with cudgels, who patrolled the streets at all hours. There were, however, some pitched battles, ending in more than a few broken heads. The neighborhood drunk tanks and guard lockups began to get longer-term guests than they were used to.

Faced with the watchfulness of the militias and the slow erosion of their numbers, the rioters came together in a huge march in the middle of the city. As the *Koskander* reported it:

SCENES OF SHAME
Rioters Flood Plaza, Tussle With Realmgold's Forces
Frustrated by their many foiled attempts to attack our dwarven and gnomish citizens, a mob of rioters marched on

Magnificence Plaza from several directions yesterday afternoon. By their appearance and demeanor, these were more of the same hired troublemakers who, this newspaper earlier revealed, have accepted pay from the rebel faction in Denning in order to import the same brand of hatred and violence into our own realm. Within the plaza, they chanted slogans and attempted to paint them on the flagstones, trees and monuments, causing much minor damage. The facade of Realmgold's House, home to several important offices of the Gryphon Clerks, was defaced and cobblestones thrown through the windows. Shops fronting onto the Plaza, including the famous Berry's eating-house, were also attacked, apparently with the aim of looting.

Acting in close coordination, military reservists from the Gulf's fishing fleet mobilized, closing in up the several roads leading to the plaza and stringing nets across them to deny the rioters egress by those routes.

Realmgold's agents then entered Realmgold's House from the rear and began to beat back the rioters with clubs. Their greater training and discipline quickly told against the larger force of their opponents, though not without injuries on the part of the brave agents.

Meanwhile, the City Guard moved up through the Great Park on the open side of the plaza, equipped with pressure-cannon which fired alternate rounds of dye and irritant gas.

Faced with this assault, the screaming criminals broke and ran, to be caught in the nets, by the agents and City Guard on the scene, or subsequently when the dye betrayed their involvement to guards on the street.

It is to be hoped that this action will see an end to the entirely manufactured unrest which has troubled us in recent days, and confirm to the rebels in Denning that Koskant wants none of their hateful philosophy.

Every Realmgold's agent in Koskant spent a night and a day sweating names out of the detainees, who filled a medium-sized warehouse in the docks district. Still coughing from the gas, still covered in the dye, rope-burned and battered and demoralized, they gave like the proverbial six-teat cow.

The Head Clerk of the Agents brought her report to Victory, swishing in triumphantly. "Got them," she said. "Young Golds from some of the highest families. Not heirs, which suggests they might have been thinking about all that land up in the beasthead country."

"This is excellent work," said Victory, looking through the report, which was, as she required, concise and to the point. "Your next steps?"

"Bring them in and see if it goes any higher, or whether they just got the money from the Denninger," she said. "Any objections?"

"None."

"What if some of the families are your supporters?"

"In that unlikely event, I will handle the problem. These people are traitors and will be dealt with as such. Let it be known through your channels — unofficially — that I consider Determined's actions in attainting his rebellious Golds fully justified. Put these youths on trial. And tell them that if they want to retain their status as Gold class and get away with merely being heavily fined and serving a long, hard sentence, they will tell you everything and name any other collaborators. Otherwise I will break them down so low that their great-grandchildren will not dare aspire to be tenant farmers on an East Province scree slope. You may quote me."

The Realmgold's tone was, as always, calm and unhurried, but she pronounced her words with a particular crisp emphasis.

The pro-Victory press somehow got hold of not only the names of the accused, but Victory's quote. The Tried and Trues struck back, running headlines like:
REALMGOLD'S CONTEMPT!
East Province Disrespected
Honest Populace Enraged
Since most of the people in East Province who could read were already Tried and Trues, though, it didn't have a great deal of impact.

The same issue of the *Gulfport Herald* ran this article:

It is alleged, by agents of the current Realmgold, that several youths of good Gold family are implicated in the recent rioting over the gnome situation. Even were this proven to be true, it would not, as rival papers suggest, imply approval by their distinguished elders of their actions.

Speaking to the *Herald* this morning, Magnanimous, Provincegold Gulfhead, son of the late Realmgold Glorious, summed up the position of other prominent Golds when he stated, "Young people are passionate about causes, and sometimes through lack of experience their passions outdistance their good sense. We all recall, I think, foolish choices made in our own youth when caught up in the excitement of the moment. While we naturally do not endorse the form of protest these young people have chosen, we do call upon the current Realmgold to give due consideration to the strong feelings aroused by her own perhaps hasty decisions concerning the gnomes, and to weigh up more carefully these consequences of her recent policies for the stability of the realm."

Victory, who had never been notably foolish, or even seemed particularly young, as far as anyone who knew her could recall, struck back with a scathingly polite opinion piece about the difference between youthful highjinks and promoting traitorous rioting against Koskander citizens for money.

Along with the names of the dead and the accounts of riots and looting — not only in the city, but also in other cities, towns and the countryside — the Denning newspapers listed the growing count of High Golds who had declared for one side or the other. Determined's intelligencers supplied him with the lists, and he sent them on anonymously to the newspapers. He judiciously delayed the lists of RBP supporters to make it seem that they were growing more slowly than they were, and once or twice added a "probable" for his side who hadn't openly declared yet, as a gentle prompt to do so. But even so, he could see the trend. It wasn't good.

General Vigilance Soldier stood at attention in front of Determined's desk, an iron-haired, steel-spined, brass-throated woman with a reputation for fierce precision. As her last name suggested, she came from an old military family which had served Denning for generations.
Determined ignored the small icicle lodged in his digestive tract and regarded her levelly. "General," he said.

"Realmgold," she said, which he supposed was a good start.

"I need to know where you stand."

"I serve the Realm and the Realmgold," she said firmly.

"Glad to hear it. Will you swear my vow?"

"I will, Realmgold."

She did, reading from the plain sheet printed with the square Dwarvish characters that were used for everyday purposes. When her copper military armring had glowed to confirm the vow, she regarded him levelly.

"I need more troops," she said.

"I'll do all I can," he said, "but unfortunately my supporters are widely spread in the outer Provinces, and most of them want to keep their troops for their own defense."

"Understood," said the general, with a crisp nod.

"I, ah, will consult with my advisors and let you know what I come up with."

The general saluted, and strode from the room.

He waited until the door closed before he started trembling.

"Victory," he said in their next scheduled session, "we need more troops."

"And I wish I could send you some of mine, but our Treaty binds us. I can no more send troops across the river than I can send them to the moon."

"At least send us more weapons."

"That I can do. I've had the manufactories running at full capacity since this business started. You'll have to send people across the river to pick them up, but they're yours whenever you're ready for them."

"We're ready for them. We now have General Vigilance, which is a weight off my mind."

"Yes, better to have her for you than against you, that's for certain. All right, I'll arrange for a shipment to be in Koslinmouth on our side of the river, and send your people the recognition codes and other arrangements."

"I, um, payment may be a little delayed, because..."

"Don't speak of it. We'll settle up when this is over. Do you want some clerks, too?"

"I'm sure Reliable would appreciate the help. Thank you."

They finished up a couple of other outstanding items, and prepared to sign off.

"My regards to the Countygold of Blueclay," said Victory. Even though her glamour was down, she had been the Realmgold, businesslike and crisp, throughout the session, and Determined found himself missing her mischievous side.

"You mean the Provincegold of Northriver."

"Isn't Tenacious Blackbluff the Provincegold of Northriver?"

"No, Tenacious Blackbluff is a traitorous weasel who has sworn to the insurgency."

"Ah. My congratulations to the new Provincegold. Well deserved." She gave him an amused and approving smile, and cut the connection.

As he deactivated the magic mirror, Determined reflected that it would be better still if Constance actually controlled any part of the Northriver province, including the County of Blueclay. Like him, she was effectively besieged in the capital.

Of the other Provincegolds, Beauty Six Gorges was firm for him, but without an external border she could do little except discourage her people from joining the rebellion.

Consolation Thousand Hills wouldn't commit one way or the other, and her countygolds were fighting among themselves. Westcoast sympathized with the RBP's ideas in general, but was too old-fashioned to go against the Realm, so he had effectively enforced neutrality throughout his province. He, at least, had a short leash on his countygolds.

Staring across the river at Koskant and dependent on its trade, Southcliffs knew better than to ally openly with the RBP, but his province had never been a strong supporter of central government and Determined's intelligencers told him that it was a source of a lot of covert support for the RBP. Felicity Lake, caught outside Lakeside Koslin when the trouble erupted, in a manor located near the heart of Silverstones' support, was using every tactic she could to delay declaring in his favor, but she couldn't last much longer. Determined nursed no illusions that she was a loyalist either, to anyone except herself, but he knew she wouldn't be able to stomach one of her countygolds telling her what to do until she was forced to it. In the absence of a declaration from her, most of her other countygolds had joined Silverstones, and the few who had declared for the Realm had been overwhelmed or were, like Felicity, prisoners in their own manors. Silverstones was, effectively, the Provincegold of Lake, and soon, thought Determined gloomily, he might well be effectively the Realmgold of Denning.

Every day, there was a trickle of new support, but every day there were more joining Silverstones than were joining the loyalist cause. Their troops began to encamp in Silverstones' county, immediately to the north of the city, and then to prevent supplies from entering. A good part of the city's trade came up the river, which Victory controlled, but too much of its food came by road to be easily replaced.

Citizens began leaving the city and joining the insurgency. Others didn't bother to leave first, but set fires and looted shops in defiance of Vigilance's troops. In Denning, Silverstones didn't have to hire petty criminals to riot. Ordinary Coppers were happy to volunteer.

Vigilance's solution when she caught them was to force them to leave by the north road. "Let him feed them, if they love him so much," was her comment.

Slowly but surely, the city was dying, and the enemy's forces came closer and closer to surrounding it.

Chapter 16: The Tussocklands

We're losing," said Determined a few days later, as he and Constance reviewed the morning's reports.

"Yes," said Constance.

"You're not going to argue with that?"

"It's the truth. Better to face it now."

"And nowhere we can get more troops. Nine curse it!"

"We could hire centaurs from Coriant."

"You fought in the Incident. You know how well that would go across."

"Sadly, yes. I blame your ancestors."

"For not making peace with the centaurs?"

"For not making themselves rulers of a united realm like Koskant. I'm afraid an appeal to national unity and asking people to support you as a strong central ruler just doesn't play well in the provinces."

"Koskant is a lot more prosperous, and smaller. But that's not important. What's important is that we're losing."

"Are you going to talk to Victory?"

"Yes, for what good it will do."

They were speaking with Victory three times a day now,

and it wasn't long before they had her on the farviewer.

She listened gravely.

"My capital is under siege," he said. "We don't have enough troops to hold it for much longer. The people are starting to get hungry, there's hardly a roof-rabbit left in the city, and I don't feel sure of their support." Old elven cities don't starve quickly, because there are gardens everywhere, on roofs and balconies, and many people raise rabbits or chickens as well as vegetables. But food still needs to come in from the country as well.

"What are you planning?" asked Victory.

"That depends," he said. "Can you send me transport ships?"

"Yes. As long as we don't land under arms, the treaty is intact."

"Then my plan is to pull out. Take any loyal troops, anyone who's openly declared for us, any and all gnomes, and whatever dwarves will come. Make the hungry people his problem." Determined had taken to not saying Silverstones' name. "If he wants the city that badly, let him have it, but on our terms. Are you prepared to host us as a government-in-exile?"

"Of course. The alliance remains."

"Then that's what we'll do. Regroup, let the people see how poor a job he does of running the country, get our internal allies to fight an underbelly war. When the chaos is at its maximum, we'll strike back hard and recapture the capital. Will you let some of your experienced troops leave your service and enter mine?"

She nodded. "Good thinking. You've been reading the Red General's history again."

Determined glanced at Constance, who was scowling.

"Constance, we're losing. You said it yourself," he said. "No shame in withdrawing and preserving what we can. Our alternative is that he breaks into the city, slaughters the gnomes and dwarves and our loyal troops and potentially you and me, and we don't have a chance to strike back later."

"I hate to abandon the people."

"So do I. But we're not, really. We're taking the loyal ones with us, and the others are abandoning us. What I hate just as much is leaving my home." He sighed. "How quickly can you get these evacuation ships to us, Victory?"

"I have the First Fleet and a collection of commercial craft belonging to me and my allies standing off or anchored in Koslinmouth, and a good few up by the beasthead lands in one inlet or another. Some even in your port. I can have them there starting tonight and ending in a couple of days. How many people do you need to move?"

"A few thousand. I'll get your clerks to do a better count and come back to you."

"I can take as many as you have. I'll talk to the beastheads and see if we can host some there temporarily, otherwise it's up and down the river as quickly as may be."

"Thank you, Victory," he said. "I hate this, you know. It's my home as well as my capital. And we're bound to lose some good people."

"Save as many as you can," she said. "The rest are not your fault, they are his."

"I doubt that will comfort their families much. But thank you."

"What about the dwarves and gnomes outside the city?" asked Constance. "And our allies?"

"Most of the dwarves and gnomes are in defensible holds," said Determined. "They've been dug in there since this started, and with the cooperation of the gnomes they can survive on cave food, fungus and blind fish, for a while, even after their stockpiles are exhausted. Their trade is almost shut down entirely, which will start to bite Silverstones before long. Any others, I've let them know which of our allies have decent castles. And I've given the same list to those allies who don't have decent castles."

"So you'll advise them to fort up and hang on?" asked Victory.

"And harass the rebels whenever possible, yes. If I must hand the realm over to Silverstones, I don't see why I should hand it over in working order."

"Well said," she said. "All right, then, I will start the fleets on their way to you as soon as may be, and we will stay in touch."

The newspapers in the capital were out of newsprint. They had shifted operations to Six Gorges, where their presses were free from RBP interference, and those newswriters stuck in Lakeside Koslin used farspeakers to file their stories, but they had no distribution within the city.

Accordingly, Reliable, with the help of Victory's clerks, had organized a system of newsrunners. Determined was impressed with the way his nervous secretary had risen to the challenges of living in a besieged city. Ever since the assassination attempt, Reliable had been taking more initiative and jumping less at sudden noises. It was as if he had come through the worst he could imagine and found courage on the other side. He worked like a gnome to organize the withdrawal from the city.

"Gnomes and dwarves get priority," he told his runners. "Then civilian humans."

"What about the military?"

"General Vigilance will instruct them." The newsrunners crouched and looked round nervously just hearing her name.

Koskant owned the Gulf, and maintained a powerful navy to escort trading ships past the notorious Corsair Coast to the south. The much smaller Denninger navy had wisely decided not to oppose them, but stayed at anchor in the Gulf port of Koslinmouth. A still smaller fleet of mainly coastal and river patrol craft was headquartered in Lakeside Koslin, and all its officers had either taken the loyalty vow or been ejected from the city.

Determined declared all fishing and pleasure craft anchored off Lakeside Koslin requisitioned for the evacuation. He wasn't going to leave anything floating there that was bigger than the buoy on a lobster pot. There were shipyards, of course, but it would take time to build any new ships.

"The problem," he said to Constance, Victory and Vigilance, "is getting everyone to Koskant."

The river was neutral territory, but the Denning bank was lined with small castles in which localgolds, or, depending on one's perspective, bandit chiefs lived and harassed shipping to the extent that they thought they could get away with it. They wouldn't attack a boat escorted by a Koskander naval vessel — Victory had broken them of this habit with characteristic thoroughness — but the river was winding, and the columns of refugees would need to be interspersed with military vessels throughout. Nor were there enough boats to take them all at once.

"Negotiations with the beastheads are not yet at a stage where they will welcome several thousand human, dwarf and gnome refugees," put in Victory. "Unfortunately."

"That leaves two possibilities," said Vigilance. "The Isle of Turfrae, or the tussocklands."

"Two problems with Turfrae," said Victory. "Firstly, it is full of Human Purity supporters. It would be out of the mud and into the quicksand. And secondly, as the old Elven Empire capital, Turfrae has symbolic importance well beyond its strategic value. Any move on the Isle will look like a play to set up as Empiregold."

"Surely nobody would think I'm taking a bunch of refugees there, having lost my own capital, in an attempt to become Empiregold," said Determined.

"Perhaps not. But they would certainly believe it of me," she said. "I'm afraid Turfrae must remain untouchable, at least for now."

"So it's the tussocklands, then."

"What about the northern coast of the Inland Sea?" asked Constance. "Forgive me, I don't know what's there."

"Not much," said Determined. "It's a swamp, actually. Filled with lizard people."

"That doesn't sound good."

"Oh, they're friendly enough to travelers, if they're approached politely. But I can't see them welcoming a mass of refugees any more than the beastheads, plus there's very little solid ground to actually put those people on, lizard folk or no lizard folk."

"The tussocklands, then," she said. "What's wrong with them? Why aren't they inhabited?"

"They are unfarmable," said Victory. "The tussock is

tough and livestock do not thrive on it, and if you burn it off the soil is rocky and infertile. But with the fishing fleet, and supplies from the beasthead country and from Koskant, refugees could live there."

"Who do the lands belong to?"

"Well, that is a nice point of international law. Under the Koskant-Denning treaty, Denning cannot claim any land south of the river, so in theory they are mine, but the Law of Habitance means that I cannot claim them unless my people have lived there self-supporting for more than five years. The beastheads have no single government to claim anything, and the only other people anywhere near are the copper elves, who stick to the forests. I doubt they want the tussocklands any more than the rest of us."

"So they're unclaimed territory?"

"Completely unclaimed. Nobody wants them, and as at this date, nobody has them."

"They sound ideal."

"Well, except for the tussock flies."

"Tussock flies," said the general.

"Yes, they bite, I am told."

"Bite? What do they eat normally?"

"Tussock birds, I imagine."

"And could we eat these tussock birds?"

"They taste unpleasantly of tussock."

"Wonderful. And, of course, the military are going to be encamped there longer than anyone."

"I keep you around for your keen ability to predict strategic situations," said Determined.

Determined had always liked brown, as a color, but he

was beginning to go off it.

The tussocklands were a dirty-looking dark brown. The tussock birds, which lived off the seeds of the tussock, were mottled various browns to blend in. The tussock flies, which abandoned the birds in droves when the humans arrived with no feathers over their biteable skin, were brownish-black. Little brown lizards lived under the tussock and ate the flies, but there weren't anything like enough lizards.

What little water there was was also brown. Fortunately it rained on the first night, and they were able to collect some rainwater in barrels, but it was going to become a problem soon. His problem, ultimately. He made a mental note to organize water shipments, if Grace, who led the Gryphon Clerks Victory had lent him, hadn't thought of it already. Based on his experience with her so far, she probably had.

"All right," he said, "lottery drawing." The Gryphon Clerks had organized the withdrawal from the capital, and they had allocated every family one of six colors and passed out dyed wooden tokens. There were six times as many people to move downriver as there were spaces in the boats that would move them, when essential personnel like the fishing families and the military were excluded. As Vigilance had predicted, the military would not be going to Koskant but staying behind, and since they were last out of the capital, everyone had been moved to a staging area in the tussocklands.

A crowd gathered to watch the drawing, clutching portable valuables and pragmatic equipment like blankets. Determined had done his best to leave little behind for the RBP, apart from such items as explosive booby-traps and caltrop spikes. He had put even more ferocious wards than usual on the royal treasury and the vaults of the city banks (after letting the withdrawing citizens put their less-portable valuables there), and they had carried away every remaining scrap of food they could.

Determined himself had packed two changes of clothes in the small trunk he allowed himself, and filled the rest of it with those books he could least stand to be parted from. The rest he had reluctantly left in place in his study. He shuddered to think of Silverstones pawing them, but there was no room in the vaults. Only the logistical skills of the Gryphon Clerks had allowed them to fit in as much as they had.

Reliable had turned a large handkerchief into a bag, which contained tokens in five of the six colors. The red tokens had already been given to the families with the youngest children, and they would go first, before the RBP had time to organize the river Golds.

Determined fumbled in the handkerchief bag and pulled the first token. "Blue!" he called out, and a mixture of cheers and groans went up. "Green!" The same.

Yellow, purple and orange followed. Reliable announced to the crowd, "We have decided to permit trading of tokens other than red tokens. To make the trades fair, we will hold a bidding session, coordinated by the Gryphon Clerks.

"Anyone who wishes to trade will register with the clerks their current token, how much they are prepared to accept for it and the value that they place on the other four token colors. They will collate the offers and announce a fair value for each token."

Directed by the clerks, people formed into lines by color. Five clerks each had a screened booth made of cloth, with five tokens, which they now laid out in the order Reliable had announced. Each person entered the booth and silently arranged the tokens on a large piece of paper which had been marked with amounts of money to indicate what they were prepared to pay or accept, and the clerks noted down the amounts and reset the tokens for the next person.

"Why are you letting them trade?" asked Constance, slapping at the omnipresent flies.

"Because they will anyway," said Determined quietly. "This way, everyone gets a fair price, if the rich want to avoid these Nine-cursed flies they pay for the privilege, and the poor can make a bit of money to take with them rather than getting to Koskant with nothing."

"Unless they're in the orange group."

"It's all right, the Gryphon Clerks and I thought of that. Without being unsubtle about it, we put mostly wealthy people in the orange group and mostly poor people in the blue group."

"And then you rigged the draw?"

"Exactly. It's easy to tell those tokens apart by feel, the paint has quite different textures."

"You have been spending far too much time with Victory."

Chapter 17: The Battle of Lakeside Koslin

Determined had his scout airboats overflying his abandoned capital at a great height, and reporting back by farspeaker, while he, Constance and Vigilance listened in.

"The opposition are slowly infiltrating the city," reported the observer. "Encountering the traps we left behind. They're going cautiously, but there's a big knot of troops outside the walls."

"Are you receiving any fire?" asked the general.

"Not as yet, General. Oh — there's the man himself."

"Their leader?" asked Determined.

"Yes, just come up in a steam carriage. He's gesturing, that's how I recognize him. Looks upset."

"I daresay."

"He just looked up at us and pointed. Looks like we're going to be receiving fire."

The pressure guns were far enough away that their popping didn't come across the link, but they could hear the commentary of the observer and the pilot.

"They can't reach us at this height," reported the observer at last. "It's higher than ideal for me, but we can still make out large troop movements. Looks like the former Countygold has got back in his steam carriage and headed off, and the troops are standing down, going back to their encampment."

"He's given up?" said Constance.

"Not likely," said Vigilance. "He'll have some plan. All right, Lieutenant, you have the farspeaker watch. Send a runner if anything happens that we need to know about."

A few hours later, a panting runner came into the tent where the three leaders were plotting strategy along with Reliable, the Gryphon Clerks, the captain of the Realmgold's guard and several senior colonels.

"General," she said, "new report from the airboats. He's using civilians."

"What?" exclaimed Determined.

"He's driving civilians into the city to activate the traps. Gnomes and dwarves, mostly, but some humans."

Vigilance swore viciously as one of the clerks tuned a farspeaker to the observer skyboats' code. "What's the situation?" she barked.

"General, they've brought in captives and they're forcing them at gunpoint into the city," came the observer's voice. Emotion roughened it and raised it half an octave from her usual smooth alto. "Hundreds of them, men, women and children."

Vigilance cursed again. "We never thought of that when we set up the booby traps," she muttered. "Should have left people behind to operate them."

"They never would have got out alive," said a colonel.

"My best people would have. Realmgold, what do you want us to do?"

"Can we mount a rescue attempt?"

"If we had more skyboats, maybe. We can't get there fast enough by water. They'd be dead before we reached them because we'd have to dodge the traps ourselves to get to them."

Vigilance paused for a heartbeat, then turned to the Gryphon Clerk at his elbow. "Grace, how quickly can we get Koskander skyboats here?"

Grace's reply was to lift her own farspeaker, adjust the setting on the code wheels and begin speaking.

"North Skybase, this is Grace Carter, Leading Clerk, at the Denninger camp in the tussocklands. My authorization is K, T, 5, S, 1, 2, 9. Get everything you have in the air and get it to me. This is Situation Hawk, I repeat, Situation Hawk. Acknowledge."

"Acknowledged, Leading Clerk, your authorization is good for Situation Hawk, we have skyboats on the way to you," said the voice at the other end. In the background, they could faintly hear another voice: "Situation Hawk, we have Situation Hawk, get your backsides in those skyboats, no sidearms, pilots only, we have Situation Hawk."

She put the farspeaker down and said to Vigilance, "We'll need gunners."

"How many?"

"Twelve."

The general nodded to a colonel, who rushed out, presumably to find a sergeant.

"Realmgold," said Grace, "do you have a coin? Anything will do."

He gestured to Reliable, who produced a two-hammer coin, and passed her the square of punched silver.

"On behalf of Realmgold Victory, I accept your purchase of the guns aboard those skyboats," said Grace. Of course, he thought, otherwise the pilots would technically be bearing Koskander arms across the border.

By the time the gunners had been assembled, the skyboats were hurtling over the horizon. Vigilance had already sent the three skyboats they had in camp with them to join the two scouts, who were trying to make the opposition troops take cover and separate them from the civilians. The twelve Gryphons did a flawless touch-and-go maneuver to pick up the Denninger gunners, who unlike Koskander gunners could enter Denning under arms, and screamed off in the direction of the city.

"They'll be there in heartbeats," said Vigilance, with some satisfaction.

Several of the Koskander skyboats carried farviewers, and they clustered around Determined's farviewer to watch the battle.

"Get the newswriters," Determined said to Reliable. "I want them to see this."

Some of the more intrepid newswriters had volunteered to come along to the tussocklands. Their papers' presses in Lakeside Koslin stood idle with no paper, but their management had bought press time in Six Gorges, and Beauty was funding their covert distribution to the other provinces.

By the time the newswriters arrived and lined up behind the High Golds, the senior officers and Grace, the skyboats had reached the city. Momentary images as they swept over the north gate showed frightened civilians of three races sheltering, as best they could, under shop awnings and behind piles of rubble. Scattered among them were the bodies of their friends and families, victims of the booby-traps they had been sent to trigger. There were also a few bodies of the soldiers who had gone in before them, identifiable by their dark-grey coats.

The soldiers who had been forcing the civilians to be living minesweepers were firing up at the Denninger skyboats, who were bravely swooping on them to draw their fire away from the civilians. One was flying askew, as if one of its flight crystals had been shattered, and one of the observers in the scout skyboats was hanging out of the hatch, dead. She must have been firing a sidearm, because the scouts mounted no guns.

The three skyboats that did have guns were now buzzing the soldiers in a circle, forcing them back from the civilians by firing on them from the front at the lowest point of their circle. As the Koskander skyboats arrived, they slipped into the circle and intensified the fire.

Behind the soldiers, steam tractors dragged heavy guns up over the broken ground to where they could target the skyboats. In the distance, a single rebel skyboat, an old, slow model, buzzed towards the battle at its inadequate top speed.

Determined spoke quietly into his farspeaker. "Fetch your Realmgold for me, please. She'll want to see this."

"She's already on her way, Realmgold," came the response.

What seemed like far too many heartbeats later, Victory's calm voice came across the link. "Determined. I am informed that we are engaged in defense of civilians at the edge of Lakeside Koslin."

"That's right," he said. "I wasn't aware that we had the option of bringing in your skyboats." His tone was hard.

"You might have been tempted to use them prematurely," she said.

"That's something we can discuss later. In the meantime, my valued ally, are there other options that I'm unaware of? In particular, are there options for evacuating these civilians who are caught between RBP troops and a series of booby-traps stretching all the way to the lake?"

She was silent for a long moment. "My apologies, Determined," she said. "I should have trusted you more fully. I can only plead a habit of not revealing all my options until they are needed. I — cannot promise that it won't happen again, but I will try to be more open with you."

"Thank you," he said, surprised by the apology.

"In answer to your question, I have three frigates with flight capability. The nearest is the *Victorious*, which is currently part of the escort for your refugee convoy. I can have it back at Lakeside Koslin within a little over an hour and a half."

"That will not be too soon," he said. "Thank you."

"I will order it immediately," she said, and he heard her speaking, away from the farspeaker, to an aide. "My apologies again, and the *Victorious* will be there soon."

He thanked her again and cut the connection.

The *Victorious*, which looked much like one of Koskant's standard waterborne frigates fitted with flight and control surfaces, touched down briefly at the tussocklands camp. The hatches sprang open, and men and women slid down ropes to the ground, heavily burdened with their personal weapons and those of the other crew members.

The ship's own weapons, temporarily Denning's for the price of a silver hammer, were left in place. Their gunners all left the ship and were replaced by Denningers, though, as were the gunners for the two additional Gryphon skyboats that the ship usually carried on its boat deck. Three of Grace's senior clerks were hauled aboard the skyboats alongside the gunners.

"We have got to get this 'under arms' clause fixed," grumbled Determined.

The tension was making him irritable. More and more artillery was coming up from the rear of the RBP forces, and more and more of the skyboats were having to detach to attack it before it could be brought to bear on them. The ever-present tussock flies weren't helping, either.

The hatches slammed and the skyship took off like a rabbit with a burning tail. Determined annoyed the other watchers by switching views back and forth between its farviewer and those of the battling skyboats during the brief interminable trip from the camp to the city.

The frigate's own Gryphons shot past it early in the flight. The involuntary civilian minesweepers were pinned down just inside the Farmers' Gate, on the north side of the city, where the North Road became the Avenue of Triumph. One of the Gryphons landed almost under the gate arch, its swiveling rapid-fire gun covering the North Road approach, while the other came almost, but not quite to rest further down the Avenue on the other side of the civilians. Its farviewer gave a ground-level, stable view of sprawled bodies and fear-filled faces, many of them far too young to be at war. Over Determined's shoulder, imagemakers clicked, capturing the moment.

"Is that a baby?" one newswriter murmured to another. A third lurched from the tent, gagging.

Determined's farspoken voice rang from the second Gryphon.

"This is your Realmgold," he said. "We are currently holding off the soldiers who attempted to force you to clear the traps we had left for them. You can safely move down Bakers' Lane into Heritage Plaza, where we will land a skyship to take you to safety. Please follow the instructions of the clerks in the skyboats." He repeated his words in his best Dwarvish. It was hesitant, and he knew he was putting in vowels that didn't belong, but apparently it was understandable, because the dwarves and gnomes among the group started moving in the indicated direction. The three clerks hopped down and began to direct them as the skyfrigate descended into the plaza and hovered above the cobblestones.

Heritage Plaza wasn't booby-trapped, because of its historic significance. It was mostly Hexagon-era elven buildings, from when the city had been an imperial port, and was itself hexagonal. The frigate landed pointing north, with its port side to the plaza entrance, and the crew flung down rope ladders from each side.

"Those who can climb, up the ladders on either side," called out the clerks. "Stay orderly. We'll help the others up." There were injured, elderly and small children among the crowd.

"Keep it moving," ordered the General. "The longer we stay engaged the more likely we are to take losses."

Already, two of the loyalist skyboats had been shot down by the RBP artillery. The pilot of the second boat, coming down in flames, still managed to retain enough control to pancake in the middle of the rebel forces. It was one of the Gryphons, and on impact it exploded, blasting shrapnel in all directions.

Determined, struggling to keep his expression calm, heard as if from a great distance Leading Clerk Grace explaining to one of the newswriters that the Gryphon skyboats didn't use propellers, like the Denninger ones, but heated air forced out of a tube. "The pilot must have jammed the energy portal open," she said. "She might have survived that crash if she'd let the safety systems cut in."

"Reliable," said Determined quietly, "find out that pilot's name. I'm going to want to name something after her later on."

"Yes, Realmgold," said Reliable in a subdued voice, making a note.

The battle raged into the evening, with Silverstones bringing up his forces as fast as he could march them. The skyfrigate had to make two trips, and the camp in the tussocklands, which had been emptying out, became newly crowded with more shocked, and often wounded, refugees. Grace produced tents and rations for them, out of the pockets in her neat Victory suit as far as Determined could tell, and the camp medics and as many Dwarvish translators as they had began to circulate.

They lost another Gryphon, though the pilot and gunner managed to bail out of this one — not before pointing it at the enemy's supply column, though. They were captured by the RBP and whisked to the back of the lines before their comrades could do anything to rescue them.

Before abandoning the field, the skyfrigate returned from its second refugee drop and made one run, at the head of a vee of skyboats, across the invading army. Rebels scattered and ran as the frigate's pressure cannons and deck-mounted fast-firing guns and the weapons of the skyboats swept over them. With Denninger gunners, not trained on the Koskander weapons, their accuracy was less than it might have been, but so large was the invading force that aiming was almost optional.

Chapter 18: Refugees

Determined had lost his city, but the rebels had paid a high price for it. Many of their troops, and even more of their artillery and other advanced weapons, had been destroyed. They had not expected the skyboats, and had brought the guns up piecemeal as fast as they could be moved from wherever they had been stationed.

The gnomes and dwarves had paid a high price too, though. As Determined walked through the camp and saw them trembling with shock, silent or weeping, children with burns and mangled limbs clinging to grieving parents or, worse, to grieving grandparents in the absence of their parents, his eyes stung.

"I need to speak to them," he told Constance.

"Is this the moment?" she asked. "They're wounded and grieving."

"Then it's exactly the moment."

He fumbled working the simple spell to amplify his voice as the second group of refugees trudged, heads down, from the skyfrigate's drop point and assembled in an open space like storm-spooked sheep.

"May I have your attention, please?" he said, his voice resonating across the tussock. Some looked up, though many of them looked down again.

"I am the Realmgold of Denning," he continued, "and I apologize for not protecting you more effectively. You have lost your homes and possessions, and more importantly you have lost friends and family, and that is a loss that cannot be set right. I promise you, though, that I am doing everything I can to restore Denning to peace and the rule of law, and when I succeed — because I will succeed — your losses will be honored and I will make right what I can.

"For now, we can offer you little but food, shelter and medical attention. Please listen to the clerks wearing the gryphon seals, they are good people and have your welfare at heart. Once again, I am very sorry you had to experience this."

An elderly dwarf, his long, braided beard matted and filthy, lifted his head and caught Determined's eye. He gave him a long look with no forgiveness in it, then turned away to organize his family and his gnomes.

"We need to get any female dwarves, in particular, under canvas as soon as we can," said Determined to Grace, who had appeared at his side. "It's a cultural belief of theirs that it's shameful for a female to be under the open sky. Please respect that."

"Yes, Realmgold," said Grace, and went to organize her clerks.

Determined, Constance and the long-suffering Reliable, along with the military personnel and anyone useful (like mages or fisherpeople), would stay in the tussocklands to the last. That was the theory.

In practice, someone had omitted to take the loyalty vow from some of the fisherpeople, and they snuck off on the second night after the battle, back to Lakeside Koslin.

Determined swore quietly when Vigilance passed on the report to him. "That means they have some boats now," he said.

"Only a few. Not enough to threaten us," she noted.

"The Koskanders didn't spot them?"

"Thought they were going night fishing."

He mulled. "We could go after them and sink them, I suppose."

The general pointedly made no comment, a response Determined had by now learned to interpret as disapproval.

"But," he added, "chasing after harmless fisherpeople and ruthlessly sinking them because they hold different political opinions is more Silverstones' style than mine."

"And a waste of resources," said Vigilance.

"And, as you say, a waste of resources. How's the red group going?"

The river convoy was in touch by farspeaker, and had reported at dawn. They had got an early start and timed their run so that most of their time in the Koslin Gorge had been during the night. The river pirates mostly operated in daylight, being devotees of the "spot a harmless-looking boat from the cliffs, launch our own boat and look threatening" school of piracy rather than the "board stealthily with rigid discipline" approach. By the time the Denning side of the river was awake, they were well down the gorge. By evening of the next day, they were in Gulfhead Province, and there were more Koskander manors overlooking them on the southern side than Denninger ones on the north.

"I told them to land in the northern counties rather than go all the way down to the port," said Vigilance. "Quicker return time for the boats."

"Good thinking," said Determined. "But how are they traveling on from there? Most of them have little children."

"Those Gryphon Clerk people have taken care of it, apparently. They're... effective."

This was high praise, coming from Vigilance. But Determined still asked the clerks what they had done.

"We've set up a tent city, Realmgold," said Grace. "Had to lean on one of the localgolds a bit."

"Why is that?"

"Not a lot of Victory supporters in rural Gulfhead Province. Their Provincegold is the leader of the Tried and True Party, which, while not quite your Realm Benefit Party, would approve of some of their ideas. Not to mention that there's already a problem with immigrants from Denning in that area."

"What kind of a problem?"

"They cross the river to look for a better life, and don't always have means of support. People won't give them jobs. They steal, sometimes. There are fights."

"So the Localgold wasn't thrilled about taking a big camp full of Denninger refugees?"

"Not exactly, no."

"How does one lean on a localgold, then?" he asked wistfully.

"We threatened him with the Realmgold's agents. The localgolds are all terrified of them."

"Why?"

"They have sweeping powers to root out corruption.

Even an honest localgold doesn't look forward to the process of being investigated, and if they're found to have been taking bribes or colluding with magistrates who do, the consequences are serious."

"Attainder?"

"In the worst cases, though the Realmgold does try to avoid that. Confiscation of the proceeds of corruption, plus fines, usually."

"Where does the money go?"

"Education. Half the Copper schools in Koskant have been founded by Golds who were offered the choice of funding a school or being reduced to the Silver class. It gives them a way to save face. Of course, if they're caught a second time..."

"That's... a remarkable system. Thank you," he said, and wandered off, deep in thought.

A little later, he was back. "So if these localgolds take bribes, how do you keep them from bribing the investigators?"

"Ah," said Grace. "That's one of the most enjoyable parts. The agents go through intensive mindmagic to increase their resistance to bribery. The penalty for attempting to bribe them is five times the amount of the bribe. Then the Realmgold awards them decorations and bonuses for successfully resisting a bribe and getting their target convicted. And they display them proudly on their clerks' lanyards, so their next target can see them."

"I imagine that would reduce the bribery rate considerably."

"Yes, those decorations are rare and highly prized."

"I only hope I get the opportunity to do that in

Denning."

"You'll be fine, Realmgold," said Grace, her round face cheerful. "Our Realmgold is on your side."

"Yes, that probably is all I need, on reflection. Thank you."

The fleet steamed back up the river at its best speed. The localgolds on the Denning bank were keeping their heads down — all those Koskander flags provoked a conditioned reaction, thanks to previous encounters — and they made good time, reaching the tussocklands again near dusk, five days after their departure. The clerks had held back some smaller craft to shuttle the holders of blue tokens southwards from the main camp, which was set up not far downstream from Lakeside Koslin. A Koskander frigate hovered protectively offshore.

Thanks to Determined and the clerks, the blue group were mostly wealthy. Grace and two of her senior clerks had gone on the frigate, along with the most influential members of the group, and as they neared shore Grace cast a voice-amplifier spell and spoke to them.

"Excuse me," she said, with polite confidence. "May I have your attention briefly, please? I have some details which will make your trip faster, safer and more convenient."

The crowd of minor Golds, wealthy dwarves and well-off human merchants regarded her with varying degrees of skepticism.

"Naturally," she continued, "the other passengers will be looking to you for leadership, so I would like to ask each of you to familiarize yourself with the simple plan that we have prepared for loading the boats to go downriver. Your swift and decisive embarkation will give confidence to the lesser passengers, and will also mean that the boats can pass the most risky part of the journey under the cover of night. You'll appreciate that delays increase the risk to everyone, so you will want to follow the plan that's already been laid out and embark as quickly as possible. We have loaded your baggage onto the boats you're scheduled to travel on, and if you get on a different boat you won't have access to it and your voyage will be less comfortable. Are there any questions about that?"

"How soon can we get back to our businesses?" asked a merchant.

"Everyone is making every effort to reduce the time of this disruption, Mistress," she said. "Part of that is to transport you to safety as quickly as we can and then bring you back as soon as possible. But while you're our guests in Koskant, we will make clerks available to you from our Office of Trade and Industry so that you can look for new opportunities to expand your business there. Yes, at the back."

"What kind of accommodation can we expect?" asked a florid-faced Gold who appeared, by his blotched and swollen complexion, to have been a favorite meal for the tussock flies. "Better than last night's, I hope?"

"There are no tussock flies where we're going, and the tents are proper pavilions," she assured him. "One has been set aside for each family or group, and naturally the location and size reflect your standing in the community. As soon as possible, we will transport you on to Gulfport or wherever else you prefer, and we are actively locating suitable premises which our Realmgold will make available to you for the duration." She had explained all this before, but she used the calming techniques that all Gryphon Clerks were taught to keep impatience out of her voice.

She fielded a couple more obvious questions, or complaints disguised as questions, and then the captain gave her a prearranged signal.

"All right, Golds, Silvers, we need to start transferring you to your designated boats now. Please come forward in the order we call your names. We will be loading Golds on the port side, that's this side, and Silvers on the starboard, and we go alphabetically." She had quailed at the thought of going in order of precedence, since not only were the precedence rules arcanely complex but someone would inevitably have been offended even if she followed them perfectly. "Can I have Gold Equanimity of Limestonecaves and party for the first boat?"

When the last drawling complaint had receded into the distance, she slumped onto a coil of rope and wiped her brow. The frigate captain walked quietly to her side and said, "Well done."

"Thank you."

"They're not used to being told what to do. They're used to being the ones who tell other people what to do."

"I know. Well, at least that's the worst of it."

The treaty between Koskant and Denning prevented Koskanders from bearing arms across the river border. As the river localgolds soon discovered, though, it didn't prevent them from firing across it when attacked.

The sun rose on several battered riverside castles, and a largely intact fleet of boats.

Chapter 19: Tempers Fray

Among Reliable's duties was fetching food for Determined and Constance. The advantage of this was that he had the opportunity to eat occasionally as well.

There was no firewood in the tussocklands. This meant that hundreds of refugees had to use military-style portable stoves, which ported in heat to warm rocks through an application of dwarven energy-magic.

The clerks had organized volunteer cooks, but many of them had little experience with such modern appliances. They were tired and traumatized, and the tussock flies were a constant distraction.

As Reliable neared the outdoor kitchen, these factors came together like a fire in a flour-mill.

A volunteer cook, slapping at a tussock fly, dropped one handle of a pot and spilled oil over the hot rocks, which she hadn't covered properly. The oil immediately caught fire, and heavy black smoke started pouring downwind, to the part of the camp where the dwarves were quartered.

Reliable heard an elderly female voice speaking irritated Dwarvish from inside a tent. As Determined had noted, dwarf women, for cultural reasons, do not go out under the sky if they can possibly avoid it. A male dwarf with an elaborately braided beard which marked him as a Craft Master emerged from the tent and headed for the source of the smoke.

Would-be helpers were pouring in from all sides, and he was jostled. His heavily accented demands for an explanation were ignored.

Reliable picked up his pace, heading for the scene, just as the first bucket of water hit the oil fire and exploded into boiling droplets in all directions. The gathering crowd screamed and de-gathered itself equally explosively. The ceramic stove cracked, spilling hot rocks onto the untidily piled supplies around it, which began to catch fire in turn. An open wooden barrel of oil had a trail of its flammable contents dripping down the side closest to the flames, and went up with a whoosh, adding more choking smoke.

The dwarf, shorter than most of the crowd, was knocked down and trampled.

His shouts brought his relatives and his gnomes out of the tent, and they began striking about them, trying to get to him. Panicked, the crowd of humans hit back.

Within a minute after the oil had hit the rocks, there was a full-blown riot in progress.

The skinny little secretary was knocked down early on. He lay winded for a moment, not thinking, just feeling, then crawled behind a tent to get out of the way of more trouble.

He clutched the ring on his right hand, the one that represented his bond with his master, and drew in a breath. A strange calm descended.

Reaching in his pocket, he pulled out a farspeaker, clicked it on, and adjusted the code wheels with deliberation. He spoke into it in a level, even voice.

"General, my apologies for disturbing you. This is Reliable, the Realmgold's secretary. There appears to be a riot in progress at the northern side of the camp, and I thought you would wish to be informed." The smoke blew into his face, just at that moment, and he added, coughing, "There is also a fire to be put out."

A riot that starts in under a minute is not so quickly brought to an end, and the same is true of a fire. Vigilance's troops were no better rested or less fly-bitten than anyone, and they had recently had to withdraw from battle and leave the enemy in possession of their realm's capital. No army likes that.

They may have been harsher with the rioters than was strictly necessary.

Determined glared across the plank on a couple of barrels which was the judicial bench at the hastily assembled inquiry.

"And so the damage reported," said Leading Clerk Grace, "amounts to: four cooking stoves cracked beyond usefulness, seven cooking pots needing new handles or distorted by heat, an unestablished number of sacks and barrels of supplies which were so extensively burnt as to be impossible to count, two tents uninhabitable because of fire, three tents uninhabitable because of riot damage, and a probably inflated number of personal possessions damaged or stolen. Twenty-three people have broken bones, including four dwarves, eight gnomes and three soldiers."

"And the claims being made?"

She handed him a long list.

He read down it in silence, then passed it to Constance, who was sitting beside him as a second magistrate.

"All right," he said. "First, let us focus on not having this happen again. What can we change to make sure it doesn't?"

"All volunteer cooks to be taught how to use the equipment properly," said the camp's military quartermaster.

"That would be a start. And don't pile gear up next to the stoves all higgledy-piggledy, neither."

"Fire drills," said the general. "And some instruction in how you fight an oil fire by smothering it, not pouring water on it."

"Language classes. Dwarvish and Pektal both," suggested a dwarf, whose Pektal was fluent enough that he had been translating for his fellow dwarves.

"And a bit more respect from the humans," muttered one of them, in Dwarvish.

"Very well," said Determined. "With the exception of that last remark made in Dwarvish, I rule that all of those suggestions be implemented by the people who made them. Grace and her people will assist." Grace gave a crisp nod. "Now, before I come to liability and compensation, I have one commendation to make. There was one person in the entire camp who kept his head, behaved sensibly and calmly and contributed substantially to resolving the situation. Reliable, very well done."

There was a small round of applause, led by Determined, Constance and Vigilance, which meant that most of the rest of those present felt obliged to join in.

"Unfortunately, my means for rewarding you are currently limited, but we will see what we can do in future. The same, I'm afraid, is true of compensation. To be frank, nobody has much money, and there's nowhere to spend it in any case. Does anyone have any suggestions?"

The Dwarvish translator spoke up. "If I may, Realmgold? In my people's tradition, if there is a fault that cannot be redressed by a fine for some reason, labour can be taken instead. I know we would appreciate some better drains and the like around our part of the camp."

"That would also," put in Vigilance, "fit neatly with traditional military punishment methods."

"That makes sense," said Determined. "Constance, do you see any point in trying to untangle the actions of individuals here?"

"Not at all," she said. "We wouldn't get a straight account if we stayed here until next year."

"Then here is my ruling. The civilian humans involved in the riot will spend a day working for the dwarves and gnomes, doing any reasonable jobs that will help their situation, in compensation for ignoring, trampling and fighting them. Those who were injured badly enough to affect their ability to work are excused, not only for practical reasons but on the grounds that their injuries constitute their punishment. The military, who used excessive force in breaking up the riot, will spend a day working for the civilians likewise. And the dwarves and gnomes, whose aggressive response contributed to the necessity of calling in the military, will spend a day working for the military, using whatever skills they have. Each group is to appoint a leader if they don't have one already, and the leaders will agree on the work to be done. If you can't agree, I will mediate, but be warned that being asked to do so will vex me. Anything to add, Constance?"

"That sounds very fair to me," she said.

"So ruled," said Determined, and rang the judicial bell that Grace had produced from wherever she got things.

Chapter 20: Meeting Victory

The bites of the tussock flies swelled up in ugly red lumps, there was a shortage of fresh water, and life under canvas was cold, damp and makeshift.

Determined, who had never been a lover of the outdoors, was sticking it out through sheer dutifulness, and secretly longing for it to all be over. He didn't quite manage to conceal his relief when Grace came to him a few days later and said, "Realmgold, I think we're going to need you in Koskant."

"Why is that?"

"We're having difficulties with the refugees, particularly the blue group." The wealthy and powerful ones, that made sense, he thought.

"What's the trouble?"

"They're not submitting to the authority of the clerks in charge of the camp."

"You may have noticed," he said, "that Denningers are not particularly good at submitting to authority. They lack practice."

"Let's hope that your opponents back in Denning are finding the same," she said. "Are you able to travel today?"

"I can be packed in twenty minutes. What about the Provincegold?"

"If you feel you need her as an adviser, by all means bring her. I'm sure she'll be as glad as any of us to be out of these wretched tussocklands."

"Yes, I think we've had adequate confirmation of why they aren't inhabited. Thank you, Grace."

When she had gone, he spoke quietly to Reliable.

"I'm going to apologize to you," he said, "and then I'm going to give you instructions. First of all, I apologize that I'm not taking you to Koskant with me, away from these cursed flies."

"You're not? I mean, yes, Realmgold."

"I need someone here that I can trust to keep order, and the General, for all her strengths, is not the person for the job. You are. All right?"

"Yes, Realmgold," said the little secretary, breaking into a smile. "Thank you, Realmgold."

Determined travelled in one skyboat, and Constance in another with Grace, since they formed between them most of the Denninger government-in-exile and couldn't both be risked in one vehicle. In the powerful skyboats, they travelled the distance from one end of the Koslin to the other in a few hours.

"A pity we can't send everyone by skyboat," remarked Constance when they reunited. "We'd be finished by now."

"If we had as many skyboats as we have waterboats, perhaps," he said.

A third skyboat descended behind them as they walked

into the camp proper, and Determined glanced round to see who was emerging. To his astonishment, it was an elegant female figure dressed all in bright white.

"Victory?" he asked.

"What? Oh," said Constance. "I believe it is."

The woman, flanked by a couple of other people who clearly had lower status, approached them in a walk that was simultaneously graceful, rapid and calm. "That's definitely Victory," said Determined. "Nobody else walks like that."

They waited until Victory caught them up, then greeted her in the manner of High Golds, each laying their right forearm along hers.

"I hadn't expected to see you here," said Determined as they walked on into the camp.

"I wanted to greet you in person," she said. "And to see how things here are progressing."

"Not very well, according to Grace."

"Ah, how are you finding Grace? Is she satisfactory?"

"She's wonderful. Are all your clerks like her?"

"She is one of the better ones," admitted Victory. "But I have several who are as good."

"Where do you find these people?" he asked, just as one of his own people — Equanimity of Limestonecaves — bustled up.

"Realmgold!" she said. "This is intolerable!"

"What's the matter, Gold Equanimity?"

"This accommodation! It's woefully inadequate. And not nearly enough is being done about moving us to something more civilized."

A Gryphon Clerk was hovering behind Equanimity with the air of a sheepdog whose sheep has just escaped and is now eating the shrubbery. She shot a look of abject apology to Victory.

"If I may?" said Victory. All eyes swiveled towards her.

"Am I to understand," she said, "that you are dissatisfied with the work of my clerks?" The words were challenging, but her tone was the quiet, even, very calm one with which Determined was becoming familiar.

Victory was wearing her gold seals, and it took Equanimity one quick glance at them to identify her. Her eyes widened and she bowed hurriedly.

"Realmgold Victory, my apologies," she said. "Your clerks have been most helpful, but I, uh, we would greatly appreciate it if, uh, it was possible to..."

"We are here, in fact, in order to hear your difficulties and come to a resolution," said Victory. "Your Realmgold will hold audience shortly. My clerks will let you know when and where."

"Oh, thank you, we do appreciate it," said Equanimity, and bowed herself away.

"How do you do that?" muttered Determined to Victory, as they began walking again.

"Methods," said Victory, equally quietly, then, at a more conversational volume, "What is that on your neck?"

He reflexively touched his neck, and couldn't keep from scratching. "Tussock fly bite."

"It looks unpleasant."

"It is."

"I'll have a healer work on it." She glanced for the merest moment at the Gryphon Clerk, who had joined them, and inclined her head slightly, and the woman shot away as if pressure-propelled from a cannon.

"There's no need..." he began.

"We cannot have the Realmgold of Denning with a big unsightly swelling on his neck," she said. The discussion was clearly closed, so he turned his attention to their destination, a large pavilion with a silver cloth gryphon the height of a man's torso sewn beside the door.

Inside was a scene of administrative industry. Gryphon Clerks came and went, or sat at folding desks in folding chairs working on papers. Victory's arrival caused barely a ripple. All the clerks glanced up almost in unison as she came through the door, putting Determined in mind of his late uncle's hunting hounds. She made eye contact with two, who stood up respectfully while the others returned to work.

"They don't bow when you come in?" murmured Determined.

"If my clerks stopped work every time I came into a room, they would never get anything done. They know who is in charge," she said. He smiled to himself.

The two Realmgolds and their entourage made their way down the central aisle between the desks to a screened-off area at the back of the pavilion. Three of the folding desks were set up in this area, forming a U shape with the opening facing the entrance.

As they settled themselves, the clerk who had left to fetch a healer returned with one, who silently set to work on Determined's neck with a salve and some kind of spell. It itched intensely for a heartbeat and then began to cool and ease, and he sighed with relief.

Victory nodded to one of her attendants, who activated a privacy rug on which the desks were set. The quiet sound of the outer office cut off abruptly. "Very good," said Victory.

"Clerk Gratitude, your report, please, before we hear from the first of the complainants."

Gratitude was the one who Determined had been thinking of as "the sheepdog clerk". She stood and gave a factual and to-the-point account of uncooperative and demanding Golds and Silvers, complaints about thievery both within the camp and at nearby farms, several minor fights and a shortage of options to transport the refugees to Gulfport. Determined glanced at Victory, seated to his right, several times during the report, but her expression was always the same. He characterized it to himself as "serene intelligence".

When Gratitude finished, Victory asked several incisive clarifying questions, thanked the clerk and handed her over to Determined. He managed to think of one or two himself before allowing her to sit down.

There was a moment of silence.

Determined turned to Victory. "I'd like to apologize," he said, "for my people's behavior."

She waved the apology away. "Let us focus rather," she said, "on solutions. Most of these problems are people problems. So let us bring in the people and talk to them. Whom shall we have first?"

"Let's have the Golds," he said. "They'll expect to be taken first, and I assume that it will take some time to fetch your local people."

"In fact, Realmgold," said Gratitude, "they have been asked to keep themselves in readiness nearby."

"Perhaps we can alternate? The most senior first?"

"Certainly, Realmgold." She stood and pushed through the canvas flap into the main part of the pavilion. Through the gap, they could see, but not hear, her instructing several junior clerks, who rushed off obediently.

Chapter 21: Complaints and Solutions

The first to be called in was the newly-created Countygold of Lakeside Koslin, Abundance Northroad. She had been a localgold just outside the city, one of the first to offer Determined her loyalty and the oath of her retainers, and had now lost not one, but two demesnes to occupation by Silverstones' forces. She had also, to a large degree, lost her newspaper, the *Eye of Lakeside*, though it continued to be printed in Six Gorges.

"Abundance," Determined greeted her. "Please sit."

"Thank you, Realmgold," she said, bowing, and seated herself in an erect, open posture.

"The Realmgold of Koskant has been kind enough to join us," Determined continued, and Abundance bowed from her seat, acceptable protocol when one had been invited to be seated by one's own liege.

"Abundance, I know you're a sensible person or I wouldn't have appointed you Countygold. What's going on here? Tell us."

"Well, it's rather a comedown for a lot of us," she said. "Admittedly much better than starving in burnt-out ruins, or in the Countygold of Upper Hills' dungeons, or lying dead in a field, which, as I keep pointing out to people, were our other options, but apart from those of us who've done military service, life under canvas is not what we're accustomed to."

"You served, didn't you?" asked Constance, knowing the answer from when she and Determined had discussed her appointment.

"Years ago, and briefly, but yes," said Abundance. "Father expected it of all of us, and especially his heir. Rightly so, too, it cultivated some good habits."

"What happened to whiners in the military?" asked Determined. He himself had not served, unusually for a Denninger High Gold.

"Lots of vegetable peeling and cleaning latrines," said Abundance. "Sadly not something we can impose on the ones here."

Determined was silent for a heartbeat, trying to work out if that was true, and reluctantly concluded that it probably was.

"If I may?" said Victory, looking at Determined. He nodded.

"These are people of ability, in some cases?" she asked.

"In some cases. There are a few dandies and wasters among them, though."

"Well, I have always found that offering appropriate responsibility to people who can handle it quietens them down nicely," she said. "Can we find them things to do around the camp? Gratitude?"

"Oh, there's plenty to do, Realmgold," said Gratitude.

"Mind you, there are some I would and some I wouldn't trust to do it right."

"Well, that is simple enough," said Victory. "If you don't trust people to do things properly, form a council and let them talk instead. They will argue among themselves, which will distract them, and if they can decide on anything at all it may well be something that does need doing."

Everyone glanced at everyone else, and Abundance let out a hearty laugh.

"Spoken from experience, it sounds like," she said. "Very good, Realmgold Victory. So the capable ones get some kind of responsibility, and the, shall we say, less capable but more audible ones get invited to be on the Camp Council."

"Will you chair it?" Determined asked her. "Not that you're less capable, quite the opposite," he hurriedly added, "but we need someone in charge who will... steer things as necessary."

"Glad to," she said.

"Very good," he said. "Why don't you and Gratitude go out into the main room and compile two lists. One of people you'd trust to be in charge of, let's say, a latrine trench detail, since we unfortunately can't set them to actually digging, and another of people who you'd like to shut in a room where they can't do much harm."

"Knew I backed the right side," said Abundance, heaving her rather bulky frame out of the chair. "Always thought you'd make a good Realmgold if you had the chance. Right, Gratitude, shall we do this? Realmgolds, Provincegold," she said, acknowledging those who outranked her as she bowed herself out.

"Well done," said Victory quietly, and Determined beamed as if she'd given him a medal. "A good choice there, I think."

"Thank you."

"Now, shall we see my Localgold? Prosperous is his name, if I recall, Localgold of Koslinbend."

Another of the clerks picked up the implied order and went to fetch the Localgold.

Localgold Prosperous Koslinbend was a gruff man in his early sixties, his face weathered by many years in the outdoors. He bowed perfunctorily to his own Realmgold and gave something that was more a nod than a bow to Determined, and an even less bow-like nod to Constance, when Victory introduced them.

He was hardly seated before he launched into a long list of complaints. Gratitude had summarized them accurately beforehand, but his list was much more detailed. Determined also noticed that in his account, in contrast to Gratitude's, none of the trouble was caused by local people. It was all initiated by the Denningers.

"...And loose gnomes in all directions," he said as he wound down. "I don't approve of this Gnome Day thing of yours, young Victory."

Victory had addressed him by his title, so calling her by her name was outright rudeness, especially when it was done so condescendingly. Her expression remained calm and unaltered.

"Localgold," she began in reply, not even stressing the title, "thank you for this opportunity to hear of your difficulties. Do you have any suggestions for what might be done to resolve them?"

"Well, you can get these northerners off my land, for a start," he said. "The Nine-cursed gnomes, too. This is a peaceful demesne, or was before they got here."

Determined remembered something Victory had said in one of their conversations. "May I?" he asked, as she had earlier. She nodded.

"Localgold Prosperous, I wonder if I can ask you something."

The localgold gave a grunt that wasn't actually "no", and Determined decided that was good enough.

"You're the northernmost inhabited demesne of Koskant, correct?"

"Correct. What's your point?"

"Our ships stopped here because it saved us time. Does anyone else do that?"

"Sometimes. Cursed sneak-ins certainly do. But there's not a lot of trade, if that's what you're asking."

"And why is that?"

"No port facilities. Just got a dock, not much of a road. Anything that comes off here is just for the local trade, because we'd have to ship it on down the river anyhow."

"And yet it seems like a reasonable landing place."

"What are you getting at, young man?"

"Well, among my people here are a number of dwarves, gnomes, some Silvers who know trade and warehousing. If we were to build you a small port, and a decent road into, say, the county town..."

The man frowned, but the angle of his head said he was listening.

"I can certainly contribute to that," said Victory. "There is a roading fund we can draw on."

"Wouldn't be too popular with Koslinmouth, would it?" said Prosperous, naming the port further downriver. His tone had lost a lot of its gruffness, Determined noticed.

"Actually, Koslinmouth is overextended and we have been searching for a solution," said Victory. "This is rather a neat one. It gives the Denningers something useful to do, it compensates you for hosting them, and it improves trade. Or will do, when we win this war."

"You think you'll win it, then?" Prosperous wasn't smiling — Determined suspected that he didn't smile often or lightly — but his tone was warming, and even edging slowly towards respect.

"Oh, yes," said Victory lightly. "No question about that. Now, the Countygold of Lakeside Koslin is just outside, meeting with my clerk Gratitude. If you tell them that the Realmgold of Denning and I have agreed to build you a port with Denninger labour and expertise, they will take care of the details."

When Prosperous had gone, Victory beamed at Determined. "You remembered!" she said.

"Find what someone really wants and find a way to give it to them that gives you what you want as well," he said. "It's excellent advice."

"And how did you think of the port?"

"Well, we flew over what there is on our way in," he said. "I thought at the time that there was potential there, but clearly there isn't much money flowing through this area. Prosperous's parents were optimists, naming him the way they did."

"Or, quite possibly, they were visionaries," said Victory. "Well played."

The rest of the day was largely consumed with taking Abundance and Gratitude's list and giving the people on it the satisfaction of hearing about their future roles from the Realmgolds, in suitably flattering terms. They also met with some of the dwarf and gnome leaders, listened to their complaints about not receiving any respect from the humans and having no useful work, and talked to them about the port, which cheered them considerably.

A lot of the complaints they heard were about living under canvas, given that the weather was deteriorating as the fallow season approached. After the third such complaint, Victory offered a solution.

"I employ a clever man to solve problems for me," she said. "We have been having difficulty building manufactories fast enough since Gnome Day, and I fortunately happened to say to him that we needed a manufactory to make manufactories. So he invented one."

"How does that work?" asked the Gold they were interviewing, intrigued. He was of what was sometimes informally called the "electrum class", Gold by birth but in trade like a Silver.

"Oh, big wooden panels, in a standard size, and they all bolt together," she said, illustrating with her hands. "He's inventing machines to go in it, too, that will make other machines, but the important part is that we can build buildings with it very quickly. We will need some for the new port. The idea is that you put up the wooden building rapidly, and then when you get time you lay bricks around the outside, unbolt the panels and take them somewhere else and start again. But we could use it to make temporary buildings that we remove altogether when we are finished with them. I will have one shipped up here, with milling tools. We will need to tell the Localgold." She glanced for a moment at one of her clerks, who nodded and scribbled notes.

As they left the pavilion at the end of the day, Determined sighed. Victory, who was walking beside him with her entourage trailing behind her, looked at him and quirked an eyebrow.

"I was just thinking of the tussock flies," he said.

"Oh, you surely aren't thinking of going back there?" she asked. "Come and be my guest in Gulfport, at least for a couple of days. The Provincegold, too."

"Oh," he said. "Oh, thank you, but I don't know if I…"

"Between us, Reliable and the General, I think we have things in hand, Realmgold Determined," said Grace from behind them.

"Oh, well, then perhaps…"

"I accept," said Constance quickly, from her position a step behind Determined and to his right.

"Very well," he said. "Thank you for your kind invitation."

Chapter 22: Getting to Know You

Determined and Constance were housed in Gulfport Castle, the official residence of the Realmgolds of Koskant for generations. It was a sprawling building, labyrinthine and confusing, but fortunately there were unused rooms just down the corridor from Victory's own.

Once they were settled and necessities provided, Determined knocked on the door of Victory's suite, as she had invited him to do. She opened the door herself, and ushered him into the tea-room he had so often seen through the farviewer. Her farviewer was set up on an easel in one corner, opposite the lemon-colored sofa.

"Come out to the balcony," she said. "The sun is out, for now."

A beautifully-carved balcony looked out across the Bay of Gulfport towards the city and the docks. They sat angled towards each other, but facing the sea, and watched the seabirds wheel and listened to their cries and the breaking of the waves. There was a powerful smell of salt, something that the freshwater lake known as the Inland Sea did not afford.

"It's both wild and peaceful at the same time," remarked Determined after a while.

"Yes. I've always had apartments facing the sea," she said. "It calms me."

He looked across at her. "It obviously works," he said. "You stayed calm all the way through that carnival of fools today."

She smiled at him, but didn't comment on his remark directly. Instead, she rose and went to a desk, simply constructed out of excellent materials, like everything else in the room, and unlocked a spell-secured drawer.

"Here is the next installment of the *Methods*," she said. "I'll ask you to keep them secure. They are not the kind of thing that should fall into the hands of, for example, people like Silverstones."

"Thank you, Victory. It means a great deal to me that you're willing to share them with me."

Before she could answer, there was a tap at the door, and Victory was called away to deal with some crisis or other. She apologized to him, saying, "Let us spend more time together tomorrow."

"I'd like that," he said.

Among the many rooms of the castle were several council chambers. Determined and Constance accompanied Victory next morning as she met with her Inner Council.

The Inner Council was headed by Amiable, the elderly Master-Mage who presided over the school of magic at the University of Illene. Amiable's face matched his name. Laugh lines patterned it like a river delta, and his eyes sparkled with good humor, but missed nothing.

Along with Amiable, Determined was introduced to Patience, the Countygold of Southern Shore, a poised-looking middle-aged woman in a steam-powered walking machine which compensated for her lack of legs; Gracious, the Deputy Chief Clerk (Victory being the Chief Clerk); and half a dozen other Gold and Silver men and women, whose names and titles he forgot almost as soon as he was introduced to them. After so many uncomfortable nights in the tussocklands, preceded by the worry of the siege, he had slept like the dead the previous night, and was still sleepy. There was a very senior Asterist scholar, and a general, but their names escaped him.

It was soon clear to Determined that the Inner Council was not a device for distracting impractical people, like the camp council Victory had proposed. It was a highly effective working body.

The main issue on the table was the Denninger civil war, but there were other items on the agenda to get through first. Victory had a party of her elite clerks in the beasthead lands negotiating a treaty, which would, if successful, eventually make those lands into a new province of Koskant. The Countygold Patience was about to fly there to conclude negotiations and represent Victory at the signing, and the current text of the treaty had to be gone over and debated. Determined thought it was a very fair treaty, but then, he reflected, he wasn't a beasthead.

Then there was the usual council business. A localgold had been caught taking bribes to give favorable verdicts in court trials, and had then threatened the investigating agent in front of a witness."

"What a pity incorrigible stupidity is not a gazetted reason for removing a localgold," remarked Victory. "Fortunately, corruption is. Give me the writ of attainder later, and I shall sign it. Is there anyone in her family we can replace her with?"

"She is almost the last of her family, Realmgold. No children, only a couple of elderly relatives," said the Deputy Chief Clerk.

"Well, then we must have a succession plan for that demesne drawn up already."

"We do, Realmgold. There are several candidates. The Countygold has a large family. And then there is a Silver in the vicinity who has a very successful manufactory, and to be honest, more influence than the Localgold already."

"Do we know anything against this Silver? Please do not tell me that was who was paying the bribes."

"To the contrary, Realmgold, he's known locally as a rigidly honest man in all his business dealings. But he's a supporter of the Tried and True party."

"What of the Countygold?"

"A loyal supporter of yours. Her second son is studying law and government at Illene, and doing well."

"So why even mention the Silver? What aren't you telling me?"

Gracious coughed. "Ah, Realmgold, the young man, the Countygold's son... he has a reputation as a bully."

"Does he, indeed. And the Silver? How does he treat his workers?"

"Better than the law requires. He sends the promising ones to school at his own expense, and has a reputation for fairness."

"Why is he a Tried and True, then?"

Determined snorted a quiet laugh at this, but nobody else joined him.

"Your predecessor's policies helped his father, and then him. And he and the Countygold don't get along."

"Because?"

"Many incidents over a number of years. I understand the worst was something to do with the Countygold's other son, her heir, refusing to marry the Silver's daughter."

"So if we appoint him, we get a localgold who's a member of the opposition faction, we perpetuate a nasty feud with his immediate liege, and we disappoint one of my loyal supporters. But he is the better man."

"That is a concise summary of the dilemma, yes."

"What would you do, Determined?" asked Victory.

He had half-expected that, but even so, it took him several heartbeats of pondering under the eyes of the council before he answered.

"The Countygold and then the Provincegold would have to approve any appointment, correct?"

"Yes, we have that practice too."

"Then I would bring both candidates in. Ask them to present their qualifications and their plans for the position. If the Silver is really the best candidate, let him show it. Investigate their backgrounds, inquire into their pasts, ask about particular incidents. See if he and the Countygold would be willing to let the past be past and work together. Ask whether he is willing to implement your policies, despite his political leanings. Then meet privately with the Countygold and the Provincegold and make a decision."

Heads nodded around the table as the council considered

this plan.

"Excellent," said Victory. "Arrange it, please, Gracious."

The Deputy Chief Clerk made a note, and they moved to the next point.

They finally came to the matter of Denning. Determined laid out the situation frankly, giving numbers of Golds and troops on both sides and describing the refugee situation in the tussocklands, and ended by thanking Victory for her help so far and asking for Koskant's further assistance.

"Before we begin the discussion, I want to say that whether or not we help Denning is not in question," said Victory. "Determined is the legitimate Realmgold, and Denning is our ally. We are obligated by treaty as well as a shared regard for the rule of law to do all we can to assist, but by that same treaty we cannot send in our own troops. We can supply weapons, we can supply logistical support, we can even supply ships, but we cannot send our own people under arms across the river."

"Is there no way to modify the treaty?" asked the general.

"That is something we plan to discuss with Master-Mage Amiable this evening," Victory said. "For now, let us take the treaty as a constraint and see what else we can manage to do."

Determined was impressed by how ready the Council were to accept that helping his realm was not negotiable. Throughout the morning's discussions, Victory had been extremely flexible and prepared to listen to alternative points of view, however far from her own, but it was clear that once she said something was not open to discussion it was not discussed.

One member of the council in particular went out of her

way to oppose anything Victory suggested, describing exactly what problems it would potentially cause. Determined began to be rather fed up with her.

"Who was that woman who kept arguing with you?" asked Determined as they left the council room. "I kept expecting you to dismiss her on the spot."

"Dismiss her? No, that's her job. She's my Adviser Against."

"You have someone whose job is to tell you not to do things?"

Victory faced her incredulous fellow Realmgold.

"My dear Determined," she said, "I command three fleets, six thousand elite clerks, and the most prosperous realm within eight million dwarfpaces. For that matter, I cannot walk down the street without seeing sixteen women wearing trousers designed to flatter my hips. It is absolutely essential that I have someone to tell me not to do things."

"What does she do if you decide to do them anyway?"

"The other half of her job, which is to work out how to keep the problems she predicted from happening, or at least reduce their impact. I find as a system it works particularly well."

Chapter 23: The Solution

After an afternoon in which they each attended to their own urgent business, the two Realmgolds dined together that evening in Victory's suite. Constance did not join them. She and the Countygold Patience, who Determined gathered was something of a right-hand woman to Victory, had formed a rapid friendship, and Constance was the Countygold's guest at her nearby manor for the evening. Master-Mage Amiable, however, was present, lighting up the room with his beaming smile.

The meal was, as Determined was coming to expect, simple, elegant and excellent. He was used to multiple servants hovering during formal dinners, and food half-cold from being fetched from a distant kitchen, but this one arrived in a wheeled cabinet pushed by Victory's personal chef. The cabinet contained both a small oven and a chiller. A timer rang a small, quiet but resonant bell when each course was ready to be eaten, and the chef would dress it rapidly and competently and serve it to them. The man's name was Faithful Cook, and Victory introduced him and said, "I have full confidence in Mister Faithful's discretion, but let us leave our discussion until after dinner regardless. His meals are not to be distracted from."

During the soup course, they chatted about the events of the day. The main meal was so good, though, that they almost stopped talking until the end. Faithful served a dessert of chilled fruit and cheese — the latter imported from the beasthead lands — packed up his cart and left them to the evening's business: the matter of the treaty.

"Let us speak Elvish," said Victory in that language. "We will be obliged to, when we speak of the technicalities of mindmagic."

Determined read Elvish fluently, but had not spent a lot of time speaking it. He nodded anyway.

"The treaty," said the old mage, in unhesitating Elvish, "is a very powerful piece of mindmagic. It's been reinforced at every accession of a new realmgold in either realm for generations, almost since the fall of the Empire. However much you might wish to revoke it, you will find yourselves incapable of doing so. A spell like that gains its own momentum. It would be like trying to break that door over your knee," he said, gesturing to the heavy oak door with its multiple layers of planks and big iron studs.

"That is not encouraging news," said Determined, focussing carefully on his adjective-noun agreement.

"I'm sorry," said the Master-Mage, "but that is how it is. All we can do is look for loopholes."

"Exactly why I had this brought up," said Victory, producing an illuminated copy of the treaty. It was the one she and Determined had signed, sealed and fingerprinted when they had renewed it after his accession.

Determined began reading it, looking for ambiguities. As

a High Gold, he had been expected to study law and mindmagic, and even in his later history studies he had spent a lot of time on laws, treaties and constitutions.

One of the exercises Victory had given him had to do with attaining a state in which possibilities are open before the mind's eye. He worked the ritual to get into that state, and noticed that the others were doing the same.

The treaty was brief, and they took it phrase by phrase.

"This is a treaty between the two realms of Denning and Koskant, for the furtherance of peace…" it began.

They discussed it for half an hour, turning phrases over and around, trying to make them fit a different way. Nothing worked.

Determined kept finding himself coming back to the first line. "This is a treaty between the two realms," he muttered. "Two realms. Why does that seem important?"

Amiable opened his mouth, but Victory gestured him to silence. Determined closed his eyes, muttering, "two realms, two realms, two…" He stopped abruptly.

After several heartbeats, his eyes flew open and he said "What if they weren't two realms?"

Two faces, already focussed on him, became even more intent, but they didn't say anything to interrupt him.

"I've never heard of this being done with realms before, mind you," he said. "But in elven law, adjoining demesnes can be combined and ruled together, at least for a period, under… certain circumstances."

"What circumstances are those?" asked the Master-Mage. Victory's tiny smile told Determined that she knew, and encouraged him to continue.

"When Golds who both hold demesnes in their own right

are oathbound as a couple," he replied. "Normally they have to be under the same higher-level liege and receive his or her permission, but in this case that's not a consideration."

"What are you saying here, exactly?" asked Victory, still smiling that tiny smile. Her glamour was up, and apart from the smile she was as unreadable as ever.

"I'm asking you, in my clumsy way, if you will be my oathmate," he said, switching back to their native Pektal.

"I accept," she said simply, and took his hand. "It's a brilliant solution."

After a long moment, during which they smiled at each other, Amiable cleared his throat.

"Well, yes, in my professional opinion, that would certainly, um, work," he said. "The treaty has centuries of momentum behind it, but if there's anything powerful enough, in the minds of the population in general, to overturn something like that, it would be the ceremony of oathbond. Good thinking, young Determined."

"Thank you, Amiable," said Victory, not breaking eye contact with Determined. "I think we should keep this quiet for now. Though I suppose we shall have to inform the Inner Council."

"Yes, indeed."

They talked out further details, and then the Master-Mage rose to leave.

"Are you going also?" asked Victory, when Determined made no move to do so.

"Oh", he said, realizing that now that they were under promise of oathbond, High Gold protocol said that he should not be in her rooms unaccompanied. He struggled to his feet.

"I look forward to seeing you tomorrow," he said.

"I also," she replied, calm and unreadable.

He left wondering what she really thought of his idea. She seemed receptive enough, but was it just a pragmatic solution to her?

He hoped not. It was more than that to him.

The Inner Council met again the following morning, and Victory bound them to secrecy and then made the announcement. Their reactions ranged from a gleeful grin and a couple of brisk handclaps from Constance, through an elegant but clearly genuine smile from Patience, to a worried frown from the Advisor Against. The last-named began to open her mouth, but Victory put up a hand.

"I don't want to hear it," she said. "Work it out." The woman nodded, frowned again in a thoughtful way, and began to scribble notes.

The Council session became a discussion of the impact of a royal oathbinding, moving by degrees into plans for the actual ceremony.

"Who is the priest going to be?" asked Determined. As heads of their respective Houses, both he and Victory were automatically priests, and would normally officiate at the oathbindings and other life ceremonies of the members of their houses and their direct vassals. For their own ceremonies, the heads of houses usually asked the next person above them in the hierarchy, but as Realmgolds they had nobody above them.

Everyone looked at Clemency, the Senior Regional Scholar of Oversight from the Asterist temple, who was expected to know the rules for such things. She did not disappoint them.

"While traditionally heads of house are oathbound under the auspices of priests who outrank them," she began, "this is not requisite under either temple or civil law. Any 'person of standing' may act, including one who is not the head of a house and thus does not usually assume priesthood." She paused meaningfully and looked directly at Victory.

Determined held his breath. Clemency was obviously suggesting herself, but the ceremony would take hours.

Victory regarded the scholar blandly and turned to the Master-Mage.

"Yes, I recall now," she said. "A favorite teacher is often chosen. Amiable, would you do us the honor?"

"It would delight me, my dear," said the old man, flashing his famous smile.

Only the Master-Mage, reflected Determined, would get away with calling Victory "my dear" in public. Then he realized that he probably could get away with it himself, now. The thought rather thrilled him.

"Good," said Victory. "All right with you, Determined?"

"Certainly," he said. It might in theory be possible to dislike the Master-Mage, he supposed, but he couldn't imagine how it would be done.

"Good," said Victory again. "Now, the witnesses."

"Traditionally," said Clemency without being asked, "these are valued and trusted friends, who…"

"Yes, quite," said Victory. "Gracious, will you stand with me? Patience is likely to be unavailable, and apart from her, I have nobody I trust more."

The Deputy Chief Clerk quivered with the honor of being asked. "Very gladly, Realmgold," he said.

Determined's choice was easy. "I believe a loyal

Provincegold would be appropriate?" he said, and smiled at Constance. She smiled back, and nodded. She was old enough to be his mother, but he considered her one of his few friends. His own mother had died when he was young, so perhaps she filled a dual role.

"How shall we ever organize this in time?" asked Gracious. "Even a Copper oathbinding is a major operation, let alone the oathbinding of two realmgolds."

"I imagine that we will have to have some sort of enormous public ceremony at some point," said Victory, with a hint of resignation in her normally imperturbable demeanor. "But we want to catch the rebel former Countygold unprepared, so it will need to be done quietly." She, like Determined, avoided saying Silverstones' name, and of course refused to use his self-granted rank of "Protector".

"Whereabouts shall we hold it?" asked Determined.

"Good point. Your side of the river is rather inaccessible just now, but if we hold it here, there is the possibility that the Denninger public will take it poorly," said Victory.

"What about on a boat in the middle of the river?" suggested Constance.

"Good thinking, Provincegold," said the Master-Mage. "Neutral territory."

"Not if the ship is Koskander," said Victory. "Can we build a barge in two parts, one on each side of the river, and float it to the centre? With a canopy, I think, and canvas sides, so that nobody can see what is going forward."

That was quickly agreed, and a rapid guest list was drawn up. The Council members, of course, all wanted to be there, and there was no good basis for excluding any of them. The hard part was going to be balancing them out with a sufficient

Denninger presence.

"I have the Provincegold of Northriver here," said Determined, "and the Countygold of Lakeside Koslin back at the camp. There are some Denninger dwarves and gnomes, too. We should include them, and some of yours."

"Quite right," said Victory. "Can your General Vigilance get away?"

"If we fly her. Why don't we invite the rest of the Golds at the camp — there aren't that many — and perhaps your gruff Localgold. I think that might be a nice gesture."

"This is going to be a big barge," noted the Adviser Against, "and a lot of people moving about. Also, a lot of important people, who are going to be in one vulnerable place. A single strike..."

"We won't tell anyone outside this room until it's time to take them all onto the barge," said Determined. "We'll say that the barge is for the port project, and take them there on the pretext of it being an inauguration ceremony."

"And we'll have every available skyboat overflying the area," said Victory.

The oathbinding, however simplified and secret, couldn't be held immediately. As soon as it occurred, word would begin to leak out, and Victory wanted to be ready to strike as soon as her troops could be ordered to cross the river. Fortunately, she already had troops gathered near the border, in anticipation of some solution being found. The longer they delayed, the more Denning suffered. Though the Denninger free press was now mostly located in Six Gorges, word was filtering in of mobs looting dwarf holds and pressing dwarves and gnomes into forced labour, and of everything from pub brawls to set-piece battles between rebels and loyalists.

Chapter 24: Briefing

Determined had ordered General Vigilance flown to Gulfport for an in-person briefing, considering the plan too important to trust to the farviewers. In a tent, even a guarded tent, a farviewer briefing could be overheard by someone outside. Even a privacy rug would do no good if someone slipped a farspeaker in.

The briefing took place in the Gulfport military compound. As well as the barracks for Victory's personal guard, this compound functioned as GHQ, and Victory assembled all of her generals (and a few other senior officers) as well as Vigilance for the briefing. She and Determined had agreed to lead it jointly.

All eyes were on Victory as they walked together to the front of the room. She had her glamour on full power, and when she reached the podium she turned and swept the room with her gaze. Everyone was already silent and attentive, but the quality of attention in the room sharpened and the military men and women sat up alertly.

"Thank you, ladies and gentlemen," Victory began. "We have gathered you here to brief you on a new development in the Denning civil war. The Realmgold of Denning and I," she gestured to Determined, and all their eyes tracked to him in unison and then fell back on Victory as if magnetized, "have come up with a means of bypassing the powerful mindmagic of the Denning-Koskant treaty and allowing Koskander troops into Denning."

Satisfied or eager expressions bloomed around the room, and Vigilance perked up, but nobody said anything or shuffled in their seats.

"Exact details will remain secret until after the solution is enacted," she continued. "What you need to know is this. I intend to support my ally of Denning with the full forces at my command. As you are aware, these forces are notably superior to those possessed by the former Countygold currently attempting to usurp the Denninger realm. My hope is that we will be able to retake the capital and the rest of Lake Province rapidly and with minimal losses on *both* sides. An extended war would be a tragedy for both realms. A war in which Denning was devastated by Koskander forces would be a significant problem for our future alliance and for public perception of their legitimate Realmgold. The usurper's forces are mostly not regular military, and they are poorly equipped and poorly trained. Poorly led, as well, I understand, since the best of the Denninger military have remained loyal to their legitimate Realmgold. Is that not so, General Vigilance?"

Determined, had he been asked, would have bet against the feasibility of Vigilance sitting any straighter than she already was, but he would have lost. She snapped out, in her best military reporting style, "Realmgold, that is correct! The Countygold's own forces are well-trained, however, and they and the Northriver forces are not to be dismissed lightly!"

"I yield to your knowledge on these points," said Victory. "In fact, our intention is to ask you to assume overall command of the operation, not only for political reasons but also because of your knowledge of the ground and opposition."

Unable to come any further to attention, Vigilance saluted.

"General Vigilance," put in Determined, "you understand our military objectives now. Would you be so good as to take over the briefing?"

"And my Koskander generals," said Victory, "please cooperate with General Vigilance in all matters. We will want to know your available strength and equipment and how quickly you can advance to staging areas, preparatory to the moment when it becomes possible to cross the Koslin under arms."

Vigilance, as she had been asked, produced several large maps in a tube and unrolled them across the briefing-room table. The officers gathered round, with the two realmgolds at one end of the table and Vigilance at the other.

"General, if I may?" said a colonel with a device of a winged eye on his collar. "These are good maps, but I can get you better ones."

"How?" asked Determined.

"Realmgold, I command the aerial mapping and surveillance corps. My people fly small one-person gliders equipped with imagemakers."

"That will be useful," said Vigilance. "But can you do it before we move?"

"Certainly, General," he said. "My fliers are unarmed. We can cross the river freely."

"Talk to me afterwards," she said. "For now, we can use these maps to plan, and I'll fill in the detail from memory. But knowing exactly where the enemy is and having a clear, up-to-date view of the terrain will be invaluable."

Over the next several hours, the generals thrashed out their strategy, with occasional insightful contributions from Victory and, Determined hoped, some not-too-idiotic questions from him. The overall plan was to bring the Koskander Second Fleet up in support of the First, which was currently blockading Lakeside Koslin, carrying as many troops as possible up from Gulfport belowdecks and out of sight. The First Fleet would then redeploy, and pick up the loyal Denninger troops from the tussocklands. Coordinating by farspeaker, the ships would land simultaneously at a number of points on the lakeshore and the upper Koslin River. They would surround the capital and also Silverstones' nearby county, plus any other area where there was a large concentration of the RBP in Lake Province. A large force would relieve the siege of Castle Lake and free the Provincegold, who would then become a political asset in attaining the surrender of her subordinate Golds.

Once the capital was surrounded on land, a second wave would attack the harbor side, with the aim being to gain the surrender of the city as quickly as possible. With the capital secured, they would then focus on capturing or killing the RBP leadership, who were assumed to be headquartered either at Silverstones Manor or in the capital itself.

As Vigilance expressed it, once the snake's head was crushed the rest would be thrashing, and with a decisive victory behind them, in possession of the capital and having the Provincegold Lake under their control, they could more easily sway the other provincegolds to declare loyalty.

"The former Provincegold of Northriver will be a problem," noted Determined. "The man's an idiot, which should make him easy to defeat, but by the same token he isn't bright enough to know when he's lost."

"If we're lucky," said Vigilance, "he'll be out of his province with the RBP leadership, and we can sweep him up with the rest of them."

"I never count on being lucky," said Victory. "Be so good as to plan for a campaign in the Northriver Province, please."

Chapter 25: Strike Against the Beastheads

"Something's going on, Protector." said Steadfast.

"What kind of thing?" asked Admirable.

"I'm not sure yet. But our spies report a lot of stirring among the recalcitrant forces."

"You still haven't got hold of their farspeaker codes?"

"Not yet. But they're building up to something, I'm positive of it."

Admirable nodded. Steadfast had worked hard to make up for his blunder over the deposed Realmgold, and was now indispensable to the integration effort. He had shown a particular aptitude for managing the idiot Provincegold of Northriver.

"Any guesses on the timing?"

"Soon, is as much as I can tell you. The weather will start to get much worse before long, and nobody wants to fight in the rain. And we're winning more counties all the time. They dare not delay."

Admirable thought for a little. "Prepare our forces. Make sure they are well-organized and dug in securely. And get Northriver out of the way." Sending him back to his province would make sure that he wasn't able to make some disastrous decision and get a regiment obliterated. "How are things going on the Isle of Turfrae?"

"Recruitment is going well. We have a shortage of arms, but the dwarves and gnomes we've captured and shipped off there are being worked day and night, and we should have at least some kind of weapon for each recruit within a few days."

"Good. Have the drills stepped up, and make sure we have enough transport boats for a strike when we need them."

Steadfast made a note. He was running out of paper in his notepad, so he made it close to the note about Northriver. On his way through the outer office, he dropped off the notes with a secretary to be transcribed and expanded into orders for Admirable to sign in bulk.

Admirable didn't believe in having a lot of paperwork or administrators, and those he had were always overworked.

Tenacious Blackbluff, who still thought of himself as Provincegold Northriver, stood in front of a full-length glass and smoothed the lines of his dark-grey RBP coat. It was definitely his color.

He turned at a knock. His secretary opened the door, paper in hand, and Tenacious opened his mouth to tell him to go away.

"Provincegold," said the secretary, before he had time to speak, "orders from the Protector himself. You're to take command of the effort on the Isle of Turfrae."

Tenacious had not been to Turfrae before. Most of the High Golds spent at least some time at the university there, but his mother, the previous Provincegold, had died when Tenacious was relatively young and he had not found the time. At least, so he always told people. In fact, he had never done well at school, so he didn't really want to go.

Being sent there to take charge of all the book-pounders, though, that suited him nicely. He endured the crossing — the lake was rough at this season — and set himself up in the best lodgings he could find in the ancient city, citing the Protector's authorization any time anyone questioned him.

Tenacious had found the time to serve in the military, and he knew how to drill troops, as per the Protector's orders. He set up a program of marching that would quickly work up to truly impressive ceremonial parades. Got them to reallocate resources to outfitting the troops with proper uniforms, too, not just the brassards that half of them had been wearing. These things were important.

His adjutant was a student, of course, though classes had been largely suspended for the duration of the emergency. One of the other student officers had a farspeaker, looted from the manor of one of the resisters whose resistance hadn't been quite effective enough, and the adjutant reported to Tenacious regularly on what had been heard over the thing. He had no idea how it worked, but it was terrifically useful.

They had an agent in place among the traders who dealt with the wretched beastheads on the southern shore, just in case the animals tried anything. A few days after Tenacious's arrival, word came from this agent that a Koskander dignitary would be arriving there soon.

"Ask him to find out who," said Tenacious. The request had to be relayed back and forth, and he had lost interest and forgotten that he'd asked the question by the time it was answered.

"Patience, Countygold Southern Shore," said the adjutant.

"What? Who?"

"That's who's arriving in the beasthead lands soon."

"So who is she?"

"I asked around among the Koskander students. She's a prominent supporter of their Realmgold. Part of her Inner Council. Ex-military of some kind, they think. Not just the military service that everyone does. Higher than that."

Tenacious put his hand on his fist and thought hard.

"She's been sent to mobilize the animals," he said at last. "They're not part of Koskant, so they can be used to invade our homeland. They hate our purity. And there are thousands of the filthy things, aren't there?"

"Many thousands, Provincegold."

"That's it, then. Prepare the troops and the transports." He stood up dynamically and decisively. "We're launching a first strike."

"Provincegold, don't you think…"

"No, I do not. I'll remind you that I was put in charge here by the Protector himself. Get it done, man!"

In all the running about that night, nobody thought to inform headquarters that they were preparing a strike on the beastheads until next morning, when the transports were already well away. And they didn't have a spare farspeaker to send with the expedition, so no matter how much Admirable ranted, there was no way of stopping it.

The wind changed direction overnight, so instead of arriving before dawn the small flotilla arrived after the beastheads — unlike Tenacious's troops — had got a good night's sleep. They were now awake and active, and quickly spotted the boats full of troops heading towards them.

The flotilla was also quite visible to the Koskander military ship standing off Snakemouth, the little village where the Snake River met the Inland Sea. It swung its pressure guns round on the boats full of troops in clearly recognizable RBP uniform, and opened fire.

Back at the Koskander military compound in Snakeport, further up the river, the commander, Captain Courageous, scrambled his troops in response to a farspeaker message from the ship. He loaded sixteen of them into the two Gryphon skyboats and dispatched them to the shore, and then led the remainder on a forced march over the intervening hill. It was covered in scrub, and there were several steep tracks, which quickly became pounded into thick, soft mud. He had his troops tear down branches from the scrubby trees to lay over the worst of it and press on.

He had had to leave the VIP, the Countygold Patience, behind in the compound, with a small force under a sergeant to protect her. He didn't anticipate any trouble, but it was as well to take precautions. She might be ex-military and High Gold, but she was in that steam-powered walking contraption, after all.

Chapter 26: The Battle of Snakemouth

Back at the coast, the fighting was fierce. One small ship, however good its armament, was not enough to keep such a large number of boats off the beach. Snakemouth lacked many good landing spots, so the boats came in until they grounded and then the troops sloshed their way to the shore, soaked up to their armpits, dragging their heavy grey coats.

While it was true that there were hundreds of thousands of beastheads in total, in Snakemouth there were fewer than three hundred. Even after their pounding by the guns of the Koskanders, the RBP forces outnumbered them, and a good many, Tenacious noted, were civilians. Most of the villagers had the heads of dogs, but there were a handful of catheads, who seemed to be leading the defense.

The catheads were armed with long spears, and with their agility and reach they would have slaughtered the invading force wholesale except that they were so few in number. As it was, a good few RBP fighters went down before they even reached the shore. The catheads didn't fight in formation, though, but individually, and the RBP were advancing roughly in lines. All that drill showing its worth, thought Tenacious with satisfaction. The catheads were pushed back rapidly into the village, where they leaped out from behind huts and terrorized the invaders as best they could until those of their enemies who carried guns were able to get in some lucky shots.

The younger and stronger of the doghead civilians had armed themselves with oars, nets, marlinspikes, fishing spears and the occasional shovel or hoe. So equipped, they opposed the landing on the beach and then, pushed back, tried to deny the enemy the village by standing shoulder-to-shoulder between their huts.

The RBP's pressure weapons, and their arrows, would have taken a terrible toll among them if they had been the only defenders. By this time, though, two skyboats were overhead, and most of the invaders armed with pressure rifles were shooting into the sky until they, in turn, came under attack from the two squads of eight that those same skyboats had dropped at either end of the beach.

Those boats that were not already sinking or stuck on offshore sandbanks came under rapid fire from the skyboat gunners, and so did anyone unfortunate enough to still be trying to make it to the shore.

Tenacious was not among these. He had not been in the first wave onto the beach, but had reached the beach among the fortunate middle group that came ashore between the advance guard, who had the catheads to deal with, and the stragglers, who faced the skyboats.

He rallied his men in the market square in the middle of the village. The small settlement had no stockade, and it was open in between the houses. The dogheads had been forced back and were fleeing into the forest at the back of the village, pursued by scattered RBP troops.

"Over that hill," shouted Tenacious in his best command voice, "lies the beastheads' main village. That is where an attack is being prepared against our beloved land. We have taken this village, we can take that one. Follow the beastheads, they will lead you straight to our goal."

They rushed after the beastheads with a roar.

Mounting a ridge, Captain Courageous met a young doghead panting with exertion, who reported in rough Pektal, "Many southerner come to village, kill, chase. They near behind us." Courageous nodded acknowledgement to him and waved his troops forwards down the slope. The force from Turfrae, unlike the Koskanders, were not actually from the south, but to the beastheads all humans were southerners, and it was not the moment to argue definitions.

Courageous and his troops started meeting more and more fleeing dogheads, some of whom tried to hide from them. He bypassed them and ran on. He wasn't as young a man as he used to be, but he trained hard and kept his people to the same standard.

He heard the popping of a pressure rifle to his right, and readied his own weapon. Rounding a corner, he came face-to-face with a human who wasn't in Koskander uniform.

He wasn't in RBP uniform either, having abandoned the heavy, hot grey coat, but he was waving a sword, and that was good enough for Courageous. He swung up his rifle and barked "Drop that weapon, soldier!"

Intensively drilled, and startled by the Koskander's sudden appearance, the soldier complied, and took a step to the side of the track as Courageous carried on straight towards him. The captain barged the younger man off the track into the scrub, cracking him under the chin with his rifle butt, and ran on. It was a calculated risk leaving a live enemy behind him, but the youth was not exactly formidable.

"Koskanders!" cried Courageous. "Form on me! Disarm enemy troops and accept their surrender!"

He could hear his people crashing about behind him and to either side, and the somewhat slower crashing from ahead as the exhausted Denningers slogged up the hill.

"Denninger troops!" he called out. "We outnumber you and we are armed with pressure weapons. Put down your arms and come forward slowly. We will not harm you if you surrender."

In point of fact, Courageous didn't know if his troops outnumbered the remaining RBP fighters, but they were positioned uphill and were grouped together rather than being spread out through the scrubby forest.

The troops they encountered first were, inevitably, the youngest and fittest, since they had come furthest up the hill. Tenacious was among them. He took pride in training with his men and keeping up with their level of fitness, and he was younger than the Koskander commander.

"Realm Benefit troops!" he cried in reply. "Form on me! Forward against the foe! Purity!"

His panting young flagbearer waved the RBP flag, and the weary troopers ignored their burning calves and pushed forward.

Bright red, with a white circle symbolizing purity, the flag stood out even in the low light under the trees. Courageous's sharpshooters fired almost in unison, and both Tenacious and his flagbearer went down.

Seeing their banner fall, the charging youths faltered, and the Koskanders' downhill rush took them down.

The train of prisoners, bound with surrender vows, trailed into the military compound at Snakeport under guard. There, they found the Countygold Patience serenely in command, a burial detail under way and another dozen soldiers, who had snuck up the river in one of the strike force's few steamboats, under surrender vow. The Countygold, it seemed, had brought a rifle, and was rather good with it. And one of the young clerks with her had been some sort of enforcer for a street gang when she was younger, Courageous gathered. He had never seen a man killed with a broken bottle before. It was unmilitary, but he couldn't argue with the result.

By the end of the day, the courtyard of the compound was packed with captured Denningers and the quartermaster was going mad trying to feed them. Courageous spoke to headquarters on the farviewer, and was surprised to get the Realmgold herself, along with the Realmgold of Denning.

"Thank you, Captain," said the latter, when Courageous had given his report. "Most of the people you captured come under the heading of 'misguided youths', and I do appreciate the fact that you took their surrender rather than wiping out a whole generation of educated Denningers. There are few enough educated people in Denning as it is."

"Thank you, Realmgold. I knew it's what our Realmgold would wish," Courageous said.

"Quite right, Courageous," said Victory. "My commendation also, and that will take more specific form once we have had all the reports and so forth. Determined, what shall we do with these prisoners?"

"I think we can issue an amnesty to most of them on the grounds that they were following what they believed to be legitimate orders. We will have to bind them with further vows to prevent them taking up arms again in the RBP cause, but once that is done I see no reason they can't return to their studies. Though I might have some words for the university authorities."

"I might have a word or two myself," said Victory. "I believe this Human Purity nonsense on Turfrae has gone on long enough. I am posting a frigate there for the duration, because I will not have them attacking us again, and I will have some of my clerks interview the faculty on Turfrae and see what they can achieve."

"Won't a move on Turfrae be... misinterpreted?" asked Determined.

"If it were the first move, yes. It is not. The first move has been made by the former Countygold of Upper Hills, and I shall make announcements accordingly."

"Which brings up a point," said Determined. "You say, Captain, that you have the former Provincegold of Northriver in custody?"

"We do. He was wounded in the battle, but he's alive."

"I'm afraid we may have to change that. I have already attainted him from his rank and position, but by taking Denningers and attacking south of the Koslin he has most grievously breached the ancient treaty between our realms, and he has participated in insurrection against my legitimate rule. I very much regret to say that he will probably have to be executed."

"Perhaps we will be able to commute that to exile," commented Victory. "In any case, Captain, please be so good as to send the former Provincegold to Gulfport. We will hold him here until Determined has his capital back and can convene a court there."

Impressed by the way the Koskanders had defended their people, only a few days later many of the beasthead leaders agreed to the proposed treaty and came under the formal protection of Koskant. The Countygold Patience was able to fly back just in time for the Realmgolds' oathbinding.

Chapter 27: Oathbinding

The day of the oathbinding dawned grey and windy.

Like any man on the day of his oathbinding, Determined was nervous and edgy, despite the self-calming exercises from Victory's little book. Between the military preparations that consumed every waking hour, the usual lack of privacy that came with the title of realmgold, and the convention that a couple approaching their oathbond were not to be alone together, he had had no opportunity to speak privately with Victory since she had agreed to be his oathmate. He had more than half convinced himself that she didn't return his feelings and was only going through with the ritual for political reasons, and it was turning his head into an ant-heap.

His valet had gone to extra trouble to make him presentable, in a new dark-green suit created by Victory's personal tailor. The tailor had struck a nice balance between the extreme simplicity of the Victory suit and Determined's more usual style. It had clean lines that made him look more imposing, as long as he didn't slump.

To keep from giving the secret away, though, and because it actually was very windy, he was wearing a cloak over the top of the suit. It blew around and was generally a nuisance. Burning away in one of the suit's pockets were a pair of diamond rings. Given the situation with the dwarves, it had not been easy to obtain matched diamond rings which were suitable for oathbinding enchantments for two realmgolds, but the Master-Mage had contacts. The old man had already set a powerful mindspell on the rings, which would intensify the oathbond.

He and Victory travelled to the venue in separate skyboats, but at the same time. The barge had been made in Koskant, in the end — it was just too hard to get part of it made in Denning — but by Denninger gnomes and humans, working together. As far as they knew, it was a floating dock to receive deliveries until the port was better equipped.

At the moment, it was drawn up to the existing wharf. Temporary steps led down to it, and the various dignitaries descended rather gingerly and made their way into the pavilion that took up almost the full length and width of the barge. The canvas sides flapped and cracked in the stiff breeze. The pilots of the two skyboats had had difficulty landing, and had to fight the wind again to take up their guard positions to either side of the barge. Out of sight, Determined knew, most of the rest of the skyfleet that wasn't immediately needed by Vigilance was circling the area and watching for any possible threat.

A Koskander patrol boat and a Denninger equivalent captained by an enthusiastic loyalist were to tow the barge out into the neutral territory mid-river. As the realmgolds arrived, Grace, who was handling the logistics, signaled the captains to get ready to pull out.

"Everyone else is here already, as planned, Realmgold,"

said Grace, her thick braid as neat as her spotless mid-grey Victory suit.

Victory nodded. "Well done, Grace," she said, and, attended by Gracious and Constance, she and Determined descended the stairs and entered the pavilion. At another signal from Grace, two lads jumped to tie down the flaps on the remaining open side.

Grace had been told the cover story as well, but she had been instructed how to prepare the room, and she was far from stupid. Determined caught her eyeing him and Victory with a subtle, and he thought approving, smile, which widened as he handed off his cloak to Reliable to hold for him and she saw the suit. Victory also passed her cloak to an attendant, but her suit was not much different from her usual appearance except for a subtle raised pattern of flowers woven into the threads. Her whole ensemble was, as ever, a brilliant white.

As the barge was towed out into midstream, the two realmgolds made their way to the centre of the pavilion, where the Master-Mage was waiting with a closed scroll-case. A few people were starting to glance at him sideways, evidently surprised that a senior mage was officiating at the inauguration of an engineering project in an out-of-the-way county. His specialty was also old elven mindmagic and lifemagic, rather than the matter-and-energy magic of the dwarves, as his wide blackwood-and-ivory arm cuff made clear even to those who didn't know him. There were some questioning glances being cast at the other members of the Inner Council, too.

The two boats towing the barge hooted their steam-horns when they reached the agreed position, and throttled down to a power level that would hold the barge in place against the current. The Master-Mage raised his arms for quiet, and the chatter in the pavilion slowly died away.

"Distinguished guests," he said in the rich, well-supported voice of a man who does a lot of chanting, "welcome. Most of you were told that you would be attending a ceremony today to mark the inauguration of work on the port here. I do apologize, but that was something of a deception."

He raised his arms again to still the surprised muttering that greeted this announcement. "I regret the misdirection, but it was necessary for security reasons. In fact, we are here for a much weightier and yet also much happier purpose." He opened an embroidered satin bag and took out the elaborately-decorated belt of an Asterist priest, marked with the constellations and with a golden buckle depicting the sun. As he belted it on, he continued, "Today we are privileged to witness the union in oathbond of Determined Stonygates, Realmgold Denning, with our own Victory Highcliffs, Realmgold Koskant."

That produced much louder muttering, some of it disapproving, though most of it, it seemed to Determined, not. The Master-Mage hushed the crowd a third time, and said, "Determined, Victory, come forward." He uncapped his scroll-case and drew out two documents, each in triplicate: the standard deed of lifebond, and a deed of union between Koskant and Denning. They were elaborately and beautifully ornamented in the ancient elven style. He set them on a waist-high pillar-like stand.

They stepped up, and each took one of his wrinkled and bony-knuckled hands, forming a triangle around the pillar. Determined, as the younger partner in a couple of equal rank, took the old man's left hand, but would be named and addressed first throughout the ceremony. This gave the person of lesser status or maturity the opportunity to refuse the oath before the more senior person had spoken.

Not that Determined was about to. He had the opportunity to regain his realm and the backing of a prosperous and extremely well-run realm to help it develop, and what was more, he got to be oathbound to Victory. His lips twisted a little as he remembered how the Advisor Against had cornered him after the announcement.

"Realmgold Determined," she had said, "I feel it's my duty to ask if you're sure about this. Realmgold Victory can be somewhat... imperious."

Determined had chuckled, and replied, "Yes, and I believe the Gulf of Koskant can also be somewhat damp. But she has another side to her that you may not have seen. I am quite sure."

Now, though, all his doubts started shouting at him at once. With anxiety tangling his gut, he made himself smile across at Victory, and she smiled back. Her glamour was at full strength, but even allowing for that, the smile made his heart kick and gave him a slowly rising hope.

"Determined to Triumph Over Adversity Stonygates, Realmgold Denning by the grace of Nine, right heritage and fair and free election, do you come here willingly to give oath of lifebond to Victory Highcliffs?" said Amiable in a clear, carrying voice. As he did so, the written version of the words he spoke, and the corresponding lines in the magical diagram between them, began to glow softly on the parchment.

Determined gritted his teeth at his full name, which he had always felt was rather grandiose, but said, "I, Determined to Triumph Over Adversity Stonygates, both in my own person and as the Realmgold Denning by the grace of Nine, right heritage and fair and free election, do most willingly come to give and receive oath of lifebond, alliance and full union to Victory Highcliffs, Realmgold Koskant."

There were a few gasps and mutters as the more politically sophisticated among the audience realized what he had just said. The Master-Mage pressed on.

"And do you, Victory Over the Threateners of the Realm Highcliffs, Provincegold Western, Realmgold Koskant by the grace of Nine, right heritage and fair and free election, come here willingly to give oath of lifebond to Determined Stonygates?"

Determined, who had not heard Victory's full name before, pressed his lips together hard and tried not to let them twist into a smile. He would definitely tease her about that later.

Victory shot him a glare which she spoiled a moment later with her own inadequately-suppressed smile. "I, Victory Over the Threateners of the Realm Highcliffs, both in my own person and as Realmgold Koskant by the grace of Nine, right heritage and fair and free election, do indeed most willingly come to give and receive oath of lifebond, alliance and full union to Determined Stonygates, Realmgold Denning."

"As you are willing, so let it be done," intoned Amiable, and joined the hands he had been holding. They joined their other hands, and spoke simultaneously to one another, beginning with each other's names.

"Victory," said Determined, "I am your lifemate. I swear to you abiding fidelity and devotion, to be linked always by oath and binding, one heart until death."

That was the personal part of the oathbinding, and he felt it take hold and link them together. He had a sudden sense of

Victory's physical presence in the room, and of her emotions, which were a combination of nervousness and excitement — and relief, coinciding with his, as they each felt the other's warm devotion. It was as if a skyhorse that had been tugging at a tether had finally slipped it, and now rose into the sky.

They shared a shy smile. The oathsense deepened and steadied as they exchanged the first pair of rings and slipped them onto their left hands, the hands of oathbond between lovers and friends.

There was more to come, though. The Master-Mage slipped the three copies of the personal oathbond underneath the other papers, which were marked with imagery of the realms of Koskant and Denning, rather than personal imagery relating to the couple.

"Realmgold Koskant," Determined continued, as Victory said "Realmgold Denning," "I am your partner and co-Realmgold. By the words of our mouths, by the will of our hearts, by the authority of our heritage and election, let our realms be one realm, united as we are united, to rule together in grace and amity while we both live, this union superseding any earlier treaty or agreement between said realms. As we will, as we speak, so it is done." They exchanged a second pair of rings, and slid them on their right middle fingers.

"As you both will, and as you both speak, so is it done and declared done," said Amiable, his voice ringing out over the flapping of the canvas and the gentle chug of the boats' engines. The crowd was silent for just a moment, then — by Victory's prearrangement — the Inner Council raised a cheer, in which the rest of the witnesses joined.

Determined hardly heard it. He had felt, like a surge in his gut, the old treaty tear loose, and had an abrupt sense of the two realms and their people as if he were looking across them from a great height and at the same time buried in them. He rocked back before locking his trembling knees. Victory, he could tell without looking, was feeling much the same, and he shared a tight smile with her.

They sealed the first trio of forms with their personal seals, Victory's gryphon and Determined's pelican, and the second with their realm seals, the sailing ship of Koskant and the spreading tree of Denning. Then they signed over the seals and fingerprinted, each muttering a personal charm as they did so. A brief glow confirmed that the documents had been magically validated.

As Amiable and the two official witnesses signed, sealed and fingerprinted in turn, the two realmgolds turned as one to the door, where Vigilance and Victory's senior general were waiting anxiously. The realmgolds nodded once, in unison, giving the order that they could not have given minutes before, and the generals saluted and left the pavilion. They would board a skyboat and depart for the north at best speed. The skyboats were equipped with farviewers, and before the ink was dry on the parchments the attack would be underway.

Determined was torn between knowing that he needed to get away himself and be involved in the command decisions, and wanting to stay with Victory.

The plan was that they would split up, he heading north to be with his people, she going back to Gulfport and the military headquarters. Before that could happen, though, there were formalities to be observed.

Pinning Senior Regional Scholar of Oversight Clemency down on what they could omit from the ceremony had taken far longer than the rite itself. However cut-down a version of a full oathbinding ceremony they were performing, though, they couldn't simply, as Victory had put it, swear and flee. They had to receive congratulations from the guests, and no Asterist oathbond ceremony could be considered complete without serving Nine Treasures Soup.

Arranging for the cursed soup had been the biggest security risk. Victory had, in the end, bound her already-loyal personal chef so stringently with a secrecy geis that the poor man could hardly speak at all.

He had, Determined had to admit, cooked an excellent Nine Treasures Soup. The three sky elements were a chicken meatball bound with egg and, he thought, something in the stock — pheasant, perhaps. The water elements were shrimps, mussels and ground-up dried seaweed, and the land elements were brassica florets, some kind of tiny squash and a distinct carrot taste in the broth. It was beautifully balanced, and there were enough of the solid "treasures" that everyone got all of them, which was considered auspicious. He took appreciative mouthfuls in between greeting guests.

The guests' reactions varied. Some, particularly the Denningers, were wary. None of them said, but he was sure all of them were thinking, "Does this mean we'll be ruled by Koskant now?" He tried to give the impression that he and Victory were equal partners, which was of course the case, at least in a legal sense, but he wasn't sure how well he was doing.

The Koskanders tended to be more positive, but then, he knew they trusted their Realmgold more than his people, even the loyal ones, trusted him. He sighed inwardly.

The big surprise was Localgold Prosperous. From their

earlier discussion, Determined had expected gruff negativity from the man, but he congratulated them enthusiastically (if still gruffly) and even choked up a little. "Excuse me," he said, "oathbond ceremonies always remind me of my own oathbond. Thirty happy years. Lost her twelve years ago come the 14th of Late Fallow." He sniffed, and turned away, clearing his throat noisily.

Finally all the guests had been spoken to, the soup had been eaten, and it was time for Determined to go. By this time, the barge had been towed back to the shore, and he and Victory walked together to the skyboat, arm in arm.

She steered him round the back of it where they could have a moment's privacy, reached up and kissed him with a pleasant thoroughness. Mouth close to his ear, she said, "When we've won, we'll have a proper celebration. Just the two of us. I own a private island in the Gulf."

"I look forward to it," he said, and embraced her hard, then climbed into the waiting skyboat. Victory stepped back, and waved as the little boat shot straight up into the wind as if flung from a catapult and then streaked for the northern horizon.

He knew she couldn't see him, but he waved back. His sense of her gradually faded as the distance between them grew.

Chapter 28: Official Announcement

Nobody had made any attempt to bind the guests at the ceremony with any kind of secrecy oath. There wasn't much point, as the first thing Victory did when she reached Gulfport was to issue a press release.

The newspapers, naturally, ran special editions as fast as they could work their presses. The *Koskander* declared:

REALMGOLD OATHBOUND!

"Closer Bond" With Denning

KOSKANT'S INFLUENCE EXPANDS

It then ran the press release virtually unaltered, followed by several pages of analysis from the usual pundits interspersed with early reports of the public reaction. The gnomes, who had been informed through their highly efficient grapevine, celebrated in the streets, carrying the famous official portrait of Victory in the traditional tugboat-shaped gnome hat which every gnome dwelling displayed beside the door. That took care of the front page image. More than a few cheering humans were visible in the crowd, as well.

The back page had a brief report of the military action in the north. Koskander forces had landed in Denning and were marching to the relief of Lakeside Koslin.

The *Gulfport Herald*, in contrast, ran the headline:

REALMGOLD OATHBOUND
Denning's Problems Now Ours
FURTHER HIT TO ECONOMY

It ran the press release too, heavily edited and editorialized on an inside page, and filled the front page with gloomy predictions of how Denning would drag Koskant down and how this "ill-advised" involvement in the Denninger civil war would be a military and economic disaster. The main picture on the front page was of damaged buildings in Lakeside Koslin, ambiguously captioned "Do We Want This?".

It wasn't complimentary about Determined, either. They chose the worst available image of him, and emphasized how he had been ejected from his own capital, how he and his predecessors had not had much effective rule outside the capital for generations, how poor and undeveloped Denning was and how immigrants from Denning had already caused problems in Koskant. "With the borders now open," the newswriter thundered, "we can expect a vast influx of these idle, ignorant thieves. In the wake of the disruption to the economy from the present Realmgold's disastrous pandering to the gnomes, will we still have a prosperous Koskant in a year from now?"

"I like how they always call you 'the present Realmgold', as if you're a temporary aberration," remarked Amiable, as the

Inner Council reviewed the press coverage together. "And how they ignore the fact that we could lose half our economic productivity and still be better off than we were under their precious Realmgold Glorious."

"Indeed," said Victory. "But we will need to put some projects in place quickly to get Denning booming. I have some ideas already."

"I'm sure you do."

"Determined and I do, I should say," she corrected herself with a small smile. "He is, if course, well-informed about his realm, even the parts where he had little practical influence, and we have drawn up a list of resources that Denning has which Koskant could use. We will want to get investors in there, perhaps offer some matching funds for quick start-ups, favorable taxation, get the people working as soon as may be. And infrastructure projects, of course."

"Then again," said the Advisor Against, "too fast a transition will create resentment in some quarters. Something more gradual…"

"The problem with a gradual transition," put in Gracious, "is that it all too easily becomes no transition at all. Look at the East Province."

"Yes, we will be taking many cautionary lessons from our East Province," said Victory. "In fact, what we have here is a grand laboratory. We have seen the effects of different policies in our six provinces here. I am sure, from what Determined tells me, that we will have a wide range of responses from the six Provincegolds of Denning. We will be able to try a number of different approaches and see which works most effectively."

"One thing I do know," said Gracious. "We'll need more

clerks."

"Yes," said Victory. "And I want to start with those students from Ancient Turfrae that we captured in the beasthead country."

Far to the north, Determined had his mind on more immediate issues, including a reluctant reacquaintance with the tussock flies. He and Constance crouched over a map beside a row of farviewers and farspeakers set up in one of the tents. Each device was carefully labelled in Grace's precise Dwarvish script with its designated code (in case the settings were altered unintentionally) and who that code connected to.

Vigilance was not in the tent, nor were Victory's generals; they were all in the field. Instead, a senior colonel from each realm sat to Determined's left, helping to coordinate communication between the different forces, and Grace's clerks scurried about assisting with the technology, fetching food and drink, taking updates to the newswriters in the next tent and generally being useful.

The newswriters were, of course, Victory's idea, and Determined had bowed to her superior experience. Himself, he would have kept them as far away as possible and told them when they'd won, but she had convinced him that it was better to involve them — as long as you were careful about what you told them.

They had farspeakers to send reports back to their papers in Koskant, and in a couple of cases in Denning. The RBP, he knew, had farspeakers too now, and were well able to listen in to the newswriters' transmissions, since the codes they had been allocated were public knowledge. Victory had taken considerable trouble to explain to him why this represented an opportunity.

Outside, most of the military were gone. Gnomes, dwarves and loyalist humans evacuated from Lakeside Koslin clustered around repeaters that passed on the words from the newswriters' farspeakers. Occasionally, a cheer or a sigh would go up in response.

Steam wagons and skyboats were still relatively rare in Denning, and even steamboats were not as common as in Koskant. Determined was therefore amazed at how quickly the Koskander forces could move. And, he reflected, if it takes me by surprise, even more so the RBP.

Just a couple of hours after the ceremony that had enabled them to bear arms north of the Koslin, the Koskanders and the Denninger loyalist troops traveling with them were close to relieving Felicity Lake. They were already drawing off the RBP forces surrounding her manor.

An unarmed Manta glider, one of the ones from the scout corps that had been mapping the potential battlefields over the past several days, had dived low over the manor at night and dropped a well-padded farviewer on a parachute into the courtyard. Felicity was on that farviewer, and one of the line of viewers in the tent was tuned to it. She had just taken the vow of loyalty, placing her troops under the authority of the realm.

"Congratulations on your oathbond, by the way, Realmgold," she said.

"Thank you, Provincegold," said Determined, not missing the use of his title. "I hope it represents a new beginning for us all."

"Not *too* new a beginning, I hope?"

"Well, of course, that is something in which, as a loyal provincegold, you will have considerable say," he said. "Within your own province, and potentially beyond."

"I must say I am very glad to hear it. I have heard that Victory is rather good at getting what she wants."

"She is a very capable woman," said Determined. "But you needn't fear that what she wants includes the overturning of established order. She's a builder, not a destroyer."

Felicity didn't respond to that, which he took as an indication of skepticism.

"Just tell me," she said, changing the subject, "when you want me to launch a sally."

"By all means," he said. "Hold hard for now. I'll hand you over to the colonels to coordinate the timing." He nodded to the clerk in charge of the devices, who turned the frame so that it was easier for Felicity to talk to the two officers.

"So Victory's military is all one structure, under the Realmgold?" Constance said quietly.

"That's right," said Determined.

"And you've laid the foundation for this half of the Realm to go the same way by declaring any loyalist force effectively a realm force."

"Yes, I have, haven't I?"

Constance considered again.

"You have my support in Northriver."

"Thank you."

"I suppose I had better get on the farspeaker to my countygolds and see if I can deliver that support. And then go and talk to them. I have to tell you, I'm dreading seeing my garden again, I'm sure it's in a state."

Determined suppressed a smile.

Constance fiddled with the settings on a farspeaker. "Nine-cursed devices," she muttered.

"That reminds me," said Determined, and dialed his farspeaker to Reliable's code to call him in from the clerks' tent.

As the dial clicked over, Reliable's voice came from the speaker.

"Excuse me," he said quietly, but with a rough edge, "what did you just say, Clerk Harmony?"

"Pardon, Mister Reliable, I was only saying that it would be a long road to get Denning to where Koskant is."

"That's not what I heard. What I heard was disrespect for my Realmgold."

"I'm sorry, Mister Reliable..."

"My Realmgold, who is also your Realmgold, the equal of Realmgold Victory."

"Well, perhaps not quite the *equal*..."

"Yes, Clerk Harmony, the equal. When you have known him as long as I have, and as *well* as I do, you will perhaps learn to respect him as the equal of any Realmgold in the world. And until you know him that well, I will thank you to keep your ignorance silent."

There was a pause, and then the very small voice of Harmony.

"Forgive me, Mister Reliable, I spoke out of turn."

"Yes, you did. Now, I have to go. I can tell through our oathbond that our Realmgold wants me."

Determined clicked the device off quietly and sat, smiling to himself, until Reliable appeared at his elbow.

Chapter 29: Not So Steadfast

Steadfast, Information Secretary of the RBP and effective second-in-command to Admirable, was worried.

As Information Secretary, he had all captured farspeakers brought to him for further distribution, and he had, naturally, held onto a couple for himself. He had, so far, been unable to get hold of any military codes, but he listened to the newswriters, and what he heard concerned him. The more so as he had checked with his people and found that the information being sent was, on the whole, reliable.

In particular, the siege of the Provincegold Lake's manor was about to be lifted by a mixed Koskander and loyalist force, and many more troops were closing in on the capital. That was confirmed.

He went to his leader and laid out the situation.

Admirable stared at Steadfast in silence for far too long. Steadfast was jumpy around him since the epic explosion when that fool Northriver had lost them the entire Turfrae reserve, and he fidgeted under his leader's gaze.

"That's not possible," Admirable said at last, quietly.

"Determined Stonygates is oathbound to the Southerner," Steadfast reiterated. "Somehow they have managed to override the ancient treaty and let Koskander troops onto Denninger soil."

Admirable heaved himself up from behind the desk, and Steadfast braced for fist-slamming and bellowing, but the Protector simply turned his back, folded his arms, and stared out the window.

There was a long, long pause, and Steadfast began to concentrate on his bladder control.

Admirable swung around and put his hands on the desk. "The capital is indefensible against a numerically superior force," he said. "We proved that ourselves. We have to get out of Lakeside Koslin. Go to ground in one of the smaller manors — mine's the first place they'd look, we can't use it. Evade their sweep, let them turn over the basket and find it empty. We have taken the capital once, we can take it again. Let them waste their troops on it. Leave it guarded as if I were here, let our troops defend it to the death, and let the Southerners be disappointed. As long as I am free the Movement will flourish and grow."

Steadfast nodded nervously and swallowed something that felt like a child's ball.

"Arrange it," said Admirable, and turned away again.

Steadfast managed to flee at a walking pace, just.

That night, with a few hand-picked guards, the two of them left the palace. They exited through a side door and joined up a few streets away with a slightly larger force that

225

had an unmarked steam carriage with curtained windows. They left the city through a secondary gate, abandoned the steam carriage short of the picket lines of the defense, now dug in around the city, and slipped through a gap which separate orders to two different commanders had created. They could see the camp lights of the Koskanders all around the city in an arc, red lanterns that let them see approaching movement without losing their night vision.

The arc was broken, though, at the Realmgold's Woods, a forest preserve which was too dense to allow a large force to move through it with any speed. A small group such as theirs, guided by someone who knew the trails, was a different matter, and they emerged near dawn at the far side.

Steadfast and Admirable had paused periodically to send and receive farspeaker messages. As far as anyone but the troops with them were concerned, they were still in the palace.

Another steam carriage met them near the woods, behind the Koskander lines, and whisked them off to a nearby manor. "Castle" would have been a more accurate term. The crossroads of Fisk had been strategic in more than one war, and Fisk Manor was well-fortified. It was also the residence of the Localgold Fisk, a woman with whom Admirable had an intimate history.

Admirable was installed in the quarters of the localgold, and despite his sleepless night appeared quite ready to welcome her unsubtly offered attentions. Steadfast left them to it, and set up initially in the small study which normally served as the administrative centre of the demesne.

He sat down, put his two farspeakers on the desk, turned one of them on and tuned it to the newswriters' reports, and rested his chin in his hands.

Provincegold Lake swears loyalty oath, is marching with joint forces on Lakeside Koslin, he heard. Provincegold Constance Northriver appears in Northgate Plaza, northern Golds swear oath. Southcliff grants free passage to Koskander and loyalist forces, Provincegold swears oath.

Steadfast had not got where he was today by being ignorant of where the meat was in the stew. He tuned the other farspeaker and gave a command concerning a package which he had left with an acquaintance, changed codes again, shut the other off and went to bed. The still-active farspeaker lay beside his pillow, where it would wake him if it made a noise.

He found the background hissing relaxing, and fell asleep more quickly than he expected.

"Realmgold," said one of the colonels a few hours later, "you need to hear this."

Determined joined the woman at her desk. She was holding a farspeaker marked "Capital Siege".

"Repeat, please," she said into it.

"We have received a note," said a man's voice at the other end. "The note gave us a farspeaker code. When we contacted it, the party at the other end claimed to be highly placed in the Realm Benefit Party and willing to help us in return for clemency."

Determined snatched the farspeaker and spoke into it. "Does this person offer any proof?"

"He claims that he can arrange a quick surrender of the capital."

"How?"

"He is well-enough placed that he can order various

commanders to maneuver, opening up gaps for us."

Determined looked at the colonel. "What do you think?"

"We need to ask the general," she said. "But if she thinks it's all right..."

"Proceed with caution," said Determined. "Make sure it's not a trap. If it's not, you can tell this person that I personally guarantee clemency."

Chapter 30: Mole

Lakeside Koslin, set between the river, the lake and several low hills, was almost impossible to defend against a determined attacker with modern weaponry. The RBP troops, mostly Copper levies who had never been in a city before, would have been quickly defeated, even had they not been betrayed.

It was certainly convenient, though, thought Vigilance, to be able to maneuver your opponent's forces as well as your own.

Time after time, she watched the most effective or best-positioned of the troops pack up and march off to defend a different spot that she had no intention of attacking, leaving the way clear to march in and capture a gate, a strongpoint or a key intersection. Her troops and the Koskanders advanced cautiously, but found no ambush, no traps, not so much as a tripwire left behind.

She reported back to Determined that the turncoat seemed to be genuine.

"Good," he said. "Give me his code. I want to talk to him."

He moved himself firmly into the commanding mindset that he had been learning from Victory's little book, and dialed a spare farspeaker to the code the General read out to him.

Steadfast had found a room in a tower where he could betray his leader without being overheard. If anyone came up the stone steps, he would hear them. Nevertheless, he crouched over the farspeaker and tended to mutter.

He had been talking to an older woman with a sharp military manner, so he was surprised when a young man's voice came from the speaker.

"Mole, do you hear me?" Mole was his codename. He had not risked exposing his true identity yet.

"I hear you. Who am I speaking to?"

"This is Realmgold Determined," said the voice. It sounded crisp and confident.

Steadfast's eyes went wide. "Hold a moment," he said, scuttled to the door and checked down the stairs quickly. Nobody was in sight.

"Realmgold, an unexpected pleasure," he said when he returned to his seat.

"Never mind that," said the young man's voice with a hint of disdain. "I want to discuss terms with you. My general tells me that your troops are maneuvering according to her orders as she passes them through you, so I'm inclined to believe you when you say you want to deal."

"I swear to you, Realmgold, I am everything I say I am."

"Swear to me, do you? Will you take the loyalty vow?"

Steadfast had to think about that. He had taken a public vow before Admirable, of course, but it had been to the people of the Movement, and in his mind preserving the lives of the soldiers drafted to defend the city was consistent with that vow. The loyalty vow, though…

"I don't know if I can, Realmgold. I am under a preexisting vow."

"That sounds like an honest answer, at least. What does your existing vow entail?"

Steadfast repeated the gist of it.

"So, you are acting to prevent the senseless slaughter of the RBP troops defending the city?"

"Yes, Realmgold. And the citizens. My sister is in the city, and her son is one of the defenders."

"Doesn't that put your leader at risk?"

"Uh, no, Realmgold. You see…" he took a breath. "The Protector and I are not in the city."

"You're not? Where are you?"

"I am… not ready to divulge our location at this time."

"But you're not in the capital? Do your troops know this?"

"No, Realmgold. They do not. I… I have been trying to think of a way to tell them that can't be traced back to me."

"Leave that to me. I have means. So, the people you contacted said that you wanted to deal for clemency. I'm listening."

"Not clemency for me only, Realmgold," said Steadfast hastily. "For the others in the Movement as well."

Determined cleared his throat. "Well. There are obvious limits. I can't simply forgive rebellion, it sets a bad precedent. Are you, by chance, Gold?"

"No, Realmgold."

"That helps. Golds are held to a higher standard. All right, for purposes of opening the negotiation: any ordinary RBP member, not one of the leadership and not a Gold, who surrenders without offering resistance will be offered the loyalty vow and, if they take it, released, with some obligation at a future time to participate in public works to restore what has been damaged in this stupid war. If subsequent investigation implicates them in acts of violence against Denninger civilians, of any race, or in other acts which would normally be considered crimes such as theft or destruction of property, they will be subject to a fair criminal trial in which their membership of the RBP shall not be considered either a mitigating factor or a reason for additional harshness. Agreeable so far?"

Steadfast considered briefly. "Agreed. What of the leadership?"

"Any Gold who has sworn to the RBP is still subject to attainder from his or her position, and may be replaced by a member of the same family, elected by that family, who is prepared to swear loyalty and place all household troops under the command of the realm. If no such person can be found, I and my co-Realmgold Victory will appoint a suitable replacement, seeking advice and so forth. Agreed?"

"Agreed." The Gold class could deal with their own problems, and he was hardly going to get a concession on that point anyway.

"In addition, any criminal acts committed or commanded by such Golds will be tried fairly in the same way as those of a Silver or Copper, and the usual penalties assessed, including fines and loss of Gold status if judged appropriate."

"Agreed."

"We're getting on so well. Now, you personally. Have you

committed any acts of violence yourself?"

"No, Realmgold. But I have passed on orders to do so, and coordinated the acts of others."

"Again, honesty. I do appreciate that, Mole. Here is my proposal. We will hold a closed hearing in which you will present a full confession of your involvement in such acts, including the names of others involved. We will investigate and confirm your story. For anything that you confess in full, you will, in gratitude for your valued assistance, be granted special clemency, meaning you will suffer no penalty. Your confession will be kept anonymous, but may be used in the trials of others. Acceptable so far?"

"What if I accidentally omit something?"

"Something we discover by subsequent investigation? My advice is that you don't do that. Do you have a good memory, Mole?"

"Yes, Realmgold," said Steadfast through a tightening throat. "Good records, too."

"Excellent. That's what I like to hear. Make sure those records get into our hands as soon as may be. Now, it has probably occurred to you that people may work out your identity based on the information available to you. I suspect you're someone highly placed, close to the former Countygold himself, and that some of what you know isn't known to many other people."

"That's correct," croaked Steadfast.

"You may find that there are attractive opportunities for someone from Denning in other parts of the world. Someone with a new identity. I believe there is a healer in Koskant who can even change the shape of the face to a degree."

"Yes, Realmgold. Thank you, Realmgold," said Steadfast

with a rush of relief.

"We will be happy to pay any reasonable relocation expenses. All clear and agreeable?"

"Yes, Realmgold. Ah... you haven't mentioned what happens to the other leaders, though. Particularly the Protector."

"The same as everyone else. Tried for any crimes they've committed, including treason. Offered the opportunity to confess, and the vow. If they take the vow, we can find things for them to do, I'm sure, helping to rebuild what they've broken, same as the Coppers. If they refuse it, they will receive the consequences of their actions."

Steadfast considered. "You don't intend to allow the Movement to continue, do you?"

"I can't."

"I... my vow is going to constrain me, Realmgold. I can't participate knowingly in the destruction of the Movement like that."

"We may be able to get that vow removed, you know."

"Let me... let me think about that."

"Do. We will have this code monitored day and night. Anything else you have to tell us will be well received."

"Thank you, Realmgold, you have been very... reasonable."

"Thank *you*, Mole. I will pass you back to the military now."

Chapter 31: In the Palace

"Right," said Determined, when he had given the farspeaker he'd been using back to the colonel. "Let's get the word out. The so-called 'Protector' has abandoned his army and snuck out of the capital. Give it to the newswriters, and get our agents in the city to start spreading the rumor. It'll be easy enough for someone to go and check, and then, I think, we'll see some surrendering."

"Do you want me to get the gliders to drop some leaflets?" asked Reliable, looking up from his notepad.

"Yes I do. Good thinking, Reliable. Draft something up based on that conversation we just had, emphasizing the advantages to be gained by surrendering peacefully and stressing that their leader has abandoned them without telling them."

Reliable scribbled a note and then called one of the clerks over and began an earnest conversation. Determined stretched, and decided that this would be a good time to call Victory for a brief chat.

In the palace in Lakeside Koslin that afternoon, a pair of

bored guards were talking in the main entryway.

"So do you reckon they'll bring back the horse racing soon?" said one.

"Bound to. Bound to. Once the horses ain't needed for the war," said his mate.

"Wish I was at the track right..." began the first. Before he could finish his sentence, the door slammed open.

The two guards were regulars in the direct service of the Protector. They had been part of his household guard when he was Countygold of Upper Hills, and they wore full dark-grey uniforms and carried pressure rifles, currently resting butt-downwards on the ground.

The mob that had burst in wore only the dark-grey brassards of irregular recruits, and bore an assortment of mostly non-projectile (and not very sharp) weaponry. Near the back, though, were a couple more regulars, who the guards recognized as the gate crew. They were shifty-eyed, as if embarrassed, but they were also frowning.

"Where be he?" cried the wild-eyed youth at the front, in a thick country accent.

"What? Who?" asked the first guard, staring at them and wondering if he should lift his rifle.

"Protector, that's who. Everyone's saying he's left city."

The guards exchanged glances.

"He's in his suite, and not to be disturbed," said the second guard.

"That's right," said the first. Absent other orders, this is what they had been told to say.

"He is like buggery," said an older peasant, and the mob rushed up the stairs.

"Hey, wait, you can't go up there. Hey!"

Reluctant to fire on their own side, the guards trailed ineffectually after the group up the marble stairs.

At the top, the leaders hesitated.

"Which way?" asked the older one, turning to the guards.

"Left, but you can't..."

They rushed off again.

"What the cursed..." began the second guard, addressing one of his colleagues from the gate. The man pulled out a flyer and shoved it into his hand, then followed the mob down the corridor.

Admirable required his guards to be literate enough to follow written orders, and the two downstairs guards bent together over the flyer and sounded out the longer words. The first, the horse-racing enthusiast, had received more practice reading because of his interest in racing form, and finished first. He lifted his head.

"Hey, wait!" he called, and hurried after the group.

The guards at the door to the Protector's suite, formerly the Realmgold's suite, were arguing with the youth and his older comrade when the downstairs guards jogged up.

"Willing, you should see this," said the first, passing the flyer forward through the crowd. The left-hand guard frowned at it, and his lips moved briefly, then his head jerked up and he stared at the racing aficionado.

"Have you heard any noise from in there today?" the downstairs guard asked.

"No, not a..." Willing, the guard, broke off and tried the door. It was unlocked.

Cautiously, gesturing the others to silence, he pushed open the leaf on his side and stuck his head into the apartment.

"Mister Steadfast?" he called tentatively. His words echoed, with the quality of sound you only get in unoccupied rooms.

"It's true," said the youth, in a whisper.

"Mister Steadfast!" bellowed Willing. "Anybody here?"

No reply.

At first cautiously, and then with increasing boldness, they entered and searched the suite. It was deserted, the desk empty of papers and the closets of clothes. They regrouped in the main room, a tea-room for entertaining.

"What are we going to do?" asked Willing.

"I'll tell you what we do," said the horse fancier. "We guard these rooms until the Realmgold gets here."

"Why don't we smash 'em up?" asked the youth.

"Because, you thistle, if we smash them up the Realmgold will find out and stick us with the bill," said Willing. "Didn't you read… never mind. We guard them, all right? We guard them until the Realmgold gets here."

"Not me," said the older of the two peasant leaders. "You lot can stand here and guard empty rooms if'n you like. I'm for telling my mates that rumors are true."

The peasants endorsed this plan, and drained from the rooms like water from a sink, leaving the regulars behind.

"Spose we better go back down to the hall," said the horse guard, scratching his head.

"Good thinking," said Willing.

They closed the door behind them with a hollow echo.

"Well," said Determined over the farviewer to Victory, late that evening, "as you can see, I'm back in my own palace again. Would you like to come up and take tea?"

She laughed. "Perhaps later in the shift-cycle. Is there much damage?"

"Surprisingly little. My books are all intact, thank Nine. They didn't get the vault open, either, though they did a lot of damage trying. The city at large is in a poor way, but not nearly as bad as it would have been without the help of our friend."

"Yes, I am of two minds whether we should even call what just happened a battle," said his oathmate.

"More like a mass surrender," he said. "Of all the things we thought we would have a shortage of, I never predicted magistrates would be one."

"Yes, how is that going?"

"Last report I got, they were still taking loyalty vows in batches of twenty." Many more than twenty people at a time would be too hard for the magistrates to monitor properly when the vow took hold. "The former Countygold of Lakeside Koslin is in her manor again, refusing to come out, and there are a few other holdouts at the guardhouses and so forth, but we can afford to just starve them out."

"Have you spoken to Mole again?"

"No, we called when we got into the palace, but he didn't answer. I suspect that his master isn't best pleased."

Chapter 32: The Protector

To say Admirable was not best pleased was an understatement.

By the time he had reappeared from the Localgold's bedchamber, where he'd slept, eaten and washed in addition to his other activities, the surrender of the city was already well underway. Steadfast took him aside and quietly informed him that the capital was lost.

"What? Already?"

"Yes, Protector, apparently there was confusion about the orders, and the opposing force is quite formidable. We have taken heavy losses and been pushed back on all sides."

This was an outright lie, but Steadfast had taken care to become the only conduit of information to Admirable, and considered he could risk it.

His leader glared at the floor. "No chance of turnaround?"

"No, Protector. The Provincegold of Lake has been relieved and is in the city even now, and Southcliffs has capitulated. We can expect no reinforcements."

Admirable paced, one hand clasping the other wrist

behind him. "Summon our retainers. We must get out of here — it's too close to the capital."

"Where shall we go, Protector?"

"I don't know!" bellowed Admirable, rounding on his minion. "You are the one who always has another clever plan. Where can we go?"

"Perhaps the west…"

"The other end of the realm?"

"Yes, Protector, but I have always felt the Provincegold Westcoast was more sympathetic than he appeared…"

"If that Nine-cursed Northern idiot had only gone where he was supposed to, we wouldn't have this problem!" shouted Admirable, leaning into Steadfast's face so that spittle struck his glasses. "That was *your fault*! This whole mess is *your fault*!"

"Yes, Protector…"

"Sniveling imbecile! Get out of my sight. And get us out of this!"

Steadfast fled. As he did so, he heard the Localgold Fisk ask, "What is it, my darling?" in her rich, sultry voice. There was a loud slap, a cry, and the sound of something soft and heavy, like the Localgold, impacting the wall. Then receding boots, and quiet sobbing.

Steadfast gave orders to the guards and retainers to prepare to leave, and sprinted up the stairs to his tower. Wheezing and gasping, he fumbled with the dials on the farspeaker. His oath was trying to hold him back, but he focussed his will and overcame it, with the help of his powerful sense of self-preservation. He wasn't going to support that madman any longer.

"This is Mole," he choked out. "The Protector is

preparing to move. Here is his location."

Arrangements took some time, and when Steadfast descended the stairs again the guards and servants were nearly ready to travel.

"Where's the Protector?" he asked.

They directed him to the study, where he found Admirable alone, writing in his journal. He could see over his leader's shoulder as he approached the desk, and read the words: "...go to seek my next appointment with that Destiny which has always guided me, and always will protect..."

He cleared his throat lightly. Admirable punctuated the sentence, capped his pen, blotted the page and closed the journal. Then he turned, and said, very quietly, "Are we ready?"

"Almost, Protector. The servants are just packing the last supplies."

"Good," he said, pocketing the small journal and standing up. "Oh, by the way, what have you done with Bounty and her household?"

"Done with them, Protector?"

"Yes, we can't have them left behind us knowing where we've gone, can we?" said Admirable, in a reasonable tone. "And we can't take them with us, they'll slow us down."

"Ah. Yes. I will arrange with the guard."

"Do so. Then join me by the stables."

Steadfast nodded and rushed out.

"Oh, Steadfast," Admirable called after him, "if you were thinking of setting the castle alight, don't. It will attract attention."

"Yes, Protector," he called back.

He seized the guard captain and drew him aside into a room. "I want you to round up the servants and the mistress and take them down to the cellar," he said. "Don't hurt them, but do it quickly. Lock them in. All right?"

"All right," said the captain, and went to leave.

"Oh, and Sharp," said Steadfast, in a very low tone, "if the Protector asks, you shot them, all right? Don't, though."

Sharp looked at him for a long moment. He held the man's gaze.

"Right," said the soldier, and went down the corridor calling for two of his men.

Steadfast exhaled slowly and went to get his trunk.

They took the same steam carriage they had come in. Most of the baggage, including Steadfast's records, was loaded into it, and Admirable and Steadfast rode inside, while one of the guards drove from the outside box. Another guard with a rifle rode beside him, and the remaining guards and a couple of servants rode horses. The servants weren't good riders, and struggled to keep up.

There was enough moon that they could see where the road was without showing a light. They headed generally west, which also meant somewhat south.

Admirable said nothing, and Steadfast reciprocated. After a while, the carriage slowed for a corner, then came to an abrupt stop.

Admirable, whose gaze had been distant, focussed on Steadfast with a speculative look. Steadfast, without a word, climbed out of the carriage, closing the door behind him, and crossed to where several of the guards were dealing with a fallen tree that was blocking the road. They had jumped their horses over the obstacle and were fastening ropes to it to tow it out of the way.

Steadfast was wearing his palest shirt and no jacket, despite the chill of the night. He stretched his arms upwards as if sleepy, locking his hands together and pushing upwards. Nothing happened, so he did it again, and this time got the result he had expected.

"I suggest you don't move," said a voice out of the darkness, followed by the sound of a number of safety catches coming off pressure-rifles in the surrounding woods. "Drop yer weapons and put yer 'ands in the air."

The guard on the carriage stood up and began to point his rifle at the voice, but before he could finish the action there were two quiet pops and he jerked and dropped dead to the ground, his rifle falling from his grasp.

"No more heroes, please," said the voice. "We're very nice to our prisoners, really."

"Lay down your weapons," said Steadfast, in a trembling voice. "We don't want the Gold to get hurt."

He winked broadly at the guard captain, hoping that the moonlight was enough to show the gesture. It must have been; the captain stared at him, then carefully laid his rifle on the ground and raised his hands. The other guards did likewise. The servants were already standing with their hands raised.

"Follow my lead," muttered Steadfast, then raised his voice.

"If you're bandits," he said, "we can pay for safe passage."

"We're not bandits," the voice said. "We're forces of the Realmgolds of Koskant and Denning, and you, my friends, are nicked."

There was a barely audible sound from inside the carriage. Steadfast's heart sank. It had sounded like a puff of air. He didn't have a personal oathbond to the Protector, who didn't like people having access to his head, but he was certain what had happened nonetheless.

"Can I... can I go to my master?" he asked, tremulously.

"Yes, get him out 'ere," said the voice, still hidden by the darkness and the woods.

Steadfast crossed and opened the door to the carriage. Admirable's body slumped out of it, and his pressure pistol dropped into the dust from his lifeless hand.

Chapter 33: Koslin

Determined very much wanted to take Victory up on her offer of an island getaway, but there was so much for both of them to do.

There were thousands of loyalty vows to administer. There were recalcitrant Golds to talk or pry or starve out of their manors. There were new Golds to appoint. There were trials to hold. There were plans to approve for the rebuilding of Lakeside Koslin.

And then there was the vast process of merging two realms into one to get underway.

Somehow, everyone made time for an all-day meeting of the new Inner Council. Beauty and Constance were on it, as were General Vigilance and Reliable. Determined was considering giving the little secretary a title that he happened to have spare. There was no shortage of those at the moment.

They were meeting in Koslinmouth, halfway between the two capitals, in a council chamber borrowed from the Provincegold of Southcliffs. Determined had expected the man to be offended by being asked to provide a meeting place for a council that excluded him, but he had taken it in good part. "I wasn't exactly quick to give my support," he admitted. "I hope I can show, over time, that you can trust me."

"I hope so too. Thank you," said Determined.

Going in arm-in-arm with Victory, Determined encountered Beauty, who bowed to them both.

"Beauty, how pleasant to see you," said Victory.

"Victory, likewise. Congratulations to you both."

Determined looked between the two women suspiciously. "Do you know each other?"

"Realmgold Victory was kind enough to assist me with some educational matters," said Beauty.

"And in return," said Victory, "Beauty was kind enough to alert me to a promising young man in Denning with whom I had interests in common. It worked out rather well."

She resumed walking towards their seats, and he accompanied her, laughing.

The first order of business was Victory's proposal that they make Koslinmouth the new joint capital. "We already have a smaller town on the Koskant shore, with room to expand," she pointed out. "It is central, and having the capital in a Denninger city will go at least a short way to easing fears of Koskander domination."

Determined had been born in Lakeside Koslin and lived there all his life. He would miss the place, despite the weather, but he could see the sense of the proposal. Apart from anything else, he didn't want to live in a different city from his oathmate. "I support that proposal," he said.

"What of the expense?" said the Advisor Against. "We are

already rebuilding Lakeside Koslin, and Gulfport has had a huge amount of money sunk into it over recent years. The Clerks' College alone…"

"Ah, yes. The Clerks' College will need expansion in any case," said Gracious. "And we have been wanting to expand to multiple sites for some time."

"The move from Gulfport can be gradual," said Victory. "You like gradual, do you not?"

"But the *expense*…"

"It is hardly as if we are scraping polish off our boots to make soup," said Victory. The Copper expression, in her precise Gold accent, made more than one of the Council blink. "Work out a budget, Gracious, and present it to us at the next meeting. And Admiration," she said to the Advisor Against, "please go over that budget beforehand and apply your worst-case predictions. Now, what's next?"

"I have calculated a ten-year schedule," said Gracious, putting up a huge piece of paper on the wall of the council chamber. The Inner Council studied it in silence with an assortment of frowns.

The Deputy Chief Clerk had drawn multiple timelines, each for some aspect of the integration of the realms. Law, the military, education and the clerks were the most prominent tracks, but the whole thing looked like a country dance for snakes.

Victory, predictably, asked the first question. "Can it be done in five?"

"I… Realmgold, I don't… that is… we can make the attempt," he conceded.

"Do," she said.

"But Realmgold, in order to do so we need to make a

great many key decisions very quickly, and the risk we then run is that powerful interests will resist the implementation of those decisions, feeling that they have not been sufficiently consulted," said the Advisor Against. "Once again, I urge a gradual approach."

"How might we mitigate the resistance?" asked Determined.

"Personal contact, I have always found, is a remarkably effective technique," said his oathmate.

"I daresay," he said drily. "One thing we need to do, then, is start putting more Koskanders and Denningers in the same room. Mix them up."

"More oathbinding," said Patience, in her crisp manner. "Get young people from both former realms in a ballroom, you'll see some communication."

"The Realmgolds have oathbound," said Constance. "Make it a fashion."

"Reliable," said Determined, "be so good as to find out how many ballrooms exist in Koslinmouth, and arrange to double that number."

"Triple," said Victory. "Though once it becomes a fashion, people will build them without our intervention."

"How do you make something a fashion?" asked Vigilance dubiously.

"You put it in the newspapers," said Victory. "Gracious, have it so arranged, please." He nodded and made a note.

"I don't quite understand," said the general.

"It's quite straightforward, General," said Patience. "You build up the balls as big events, so that people are honored to be invited. Only invite the High Gold families, at first, then slowly work down. You make sure plenty of newswriters are there, with imagetakers so that people get their pictures in the newspaper and boast to their friends. If any oathbonds result, you make sure that gets in the newspaper, too. Over time, you create a perception: Meeting people from the other realm is exciting and interesting. Oathbonds with people from the other realm are happening more and more, and what's more, if you have one you'll be feted for it."

"And once the Golds are doing it, the Silvers will want to do it, and there are more of them," noted Victory. "It becomes, therefore, a fashion."

"And this, in turn, creates demand for travel between the realms to be made easier, which makes those projects easier to sell," said Gracious. He made a note on his chart.

"Better transport leads to more trade, of course, meaning there is more money and more work. Plus people start traveling and relocating to where the work is, mixing the populations even more," Victory continued.

"By a similar process, we make the same artists and musicians and plays and books fashionable in both countries, and people have more in common to talk about," said Patience.

"Preferably works about how the two realms have a lot in common?" asked Determined.

"Not necessarily. Comedies about how they're different will work just as well," said Victory. "And as more and more people marry across the realms, there will be plenty of material for comedy, you can be sure. But everyone will be laughing together."

"A realm unified by young people dancing with each other, getting oathbound, and then laughing at the results," said Vigilance. She still sounded dubious, but she was smiling.

"Better than sending in troops, I suppose."

"Much better. Cheaper, also," said Victory. "Always better to have someone else do the bulk of the work, if you can."

"So what are we calling this new united realm?" asked Vigilance. "Koskant and Denning? Denning and Koskant?"

"I think we need a new name entirely," said the Master-Mage. "Start fresh."

"Koslin," said Reliable. Everyone looked at him, and he blushed. "After the river. It used to be the border, now it runs down the middle."

"Symbolically turning what divided us into what unites us. I like it," Master-Mage Amiable said.

The proposal passed by unanimous vote.

Gracious was reporting on his proposals for fielding more clerks by recalling those who had failed the ferocious exams and giving them another chance when Victory passed Determined a note.

Island tomorrow? it said in her elegant Elvish script.

He turned it over and scribbled on the back, *Love to, but can we get away?*

She read it and wrote underneath, *We are the Realmgolds. We tell people what is going to happen.*

He smiled and pocketed the note.

Chapter 34: Island

The session ran late into the evening. As they escaped at last down a back corridor outside the council chamber, Determined asked, "How long does it take to get to this island?"

"It's a long way out in the gulf. Even flying, we won't be there until morning."

His heart sank. The Inner Council had insisted that the joint Realmgolds not travel in the same vehicle at any time. He was going to have a long, lonely flight.

She stopped and, unusually for Victory, put her arms around him and hugged him. "Don't worry. Tomorrow will make up for it."

He looked down into her eyes. She had dropped the glamour once they were out of sight of the council, and he could see how tired she was, but there was a mischievous sparkle that the dignified Realmgold never allowed herself.

"Oh?" he said.

"Well, we may be oathbound for political reasons, but that's no reason why we shouldn't enjoy it," she said, stood up on her toes and kissed him lightly. "Come on."

She took his hand, and they scampered down the stairs side by side.

Outside, it was raining, increasingly heavily. Victory had arranged for their skyboats to pick them up from the courtyard, and they dashed across the intervening space. He boosted her into her boat, and she turned and waved him off.

"Get out of the rain!" she called. He nodded, and hurried to his boat. The passenger compartment had been reconfigured into a bed of sorts by hanging a canvas sling. Used to sleeping in the conditions of the tussocklands, he found it comfortable enough.

"Evening, Brightness," he said to his pilot.

"Evening, Realmgold. There's a towel there somewhere if you need it."

"Thanks. You know where you're going?"

"Just following Friendship there. But yes, I have a map if I need it."

"Good. I'm going to try to get some sleep."

"Good idea," said Brightness, and pulled a curtain between them. "Call out if you need anything."

He mopped himself with the towel, lay down, and practiced the Third Ritual of Sleep. Then practiced it again. Sometime during his third attempt, he fell asleep.

He woke with a start as the outside door opened and Brightness peered in. It was morning, and behind the pilot he could see a sandy beach and a grey winter sea. He blinked.

"We're there?" he asked.

"Yes, Realmgold. Sleep well?"

"Surprisingly well. Thanks for a smooth flight." He

stretched and maneuvered himself out of the compartment.

"I'll bring your bag up," said Brightness. "The Realmgold, uh, Realmgold Victory is waiting for you."

In front of the pilots, Victory had her glamour up — nobody but Determined ever saw her without it — so it was hard to tell whether she had slept well or not. She greeted him cheerfully, though formally, and they linked arms and walked across a springy lawn to a small manor.

"This belongs to my family," she said. "Not to the Realm or even the Province. I keep a very small staff here, and use it for important private conferences."

"Such as the one we're about to have?" he asked, straight-faced.

"Well, this one will be special," she admitted. "The first such conference, but I hope not the last."

"I hope so too," he said, and she squeezed his arm.

"The Master-Mage has excelled himself with these rings," he said. "Even with your glamour on, when we touch, I know what you're feeling."

They walked on for a few steps.

"Right now, for example," he said, "you're blushing."

Breakfast was set out inside, buffet-style. First, though, they greeted the staff, an elderly couple, who bowed and led them to separate washrooms, then effaced themselves, going to see to the pilots.

Victory returned having taken down her hair, which she normally wore in a braid piled on top of her head, and brushed it out. It reached almost to the small of her back. It made her look younger, and not at all like the Realmgold.

"The pilots will be in the staff wing," said Victory, when

they had served themselves breakfast and were seated at the table eating. "We are in this wing," she gestured to her right. "Very private."

"Good," said Determined.

Now that her glamour was down, he could see that she looked tired, but no more so than usual. She smiled brightly at him.

"Once we've eaten, I thought I might show you the library," she said.

"The library?"

"Yes, I know how much you love books, and there's a very fine old one in particular I'd like you to look at." That mischief was dancing in her eyes again. He smiled back, not understanding but trusting that whatever surprise she had for him was one he'd enjoy.

They finished their light breakfast and she led him down the hall into the private wing.

"Through here," she said, opening a large, heavy door.

For such a small manor, it did, in fact, have an impressive library. It was compact, but there were at least as many books here as in his study back at the palace in Lakeside Koslin. They were neatly organized in plain, dark bookcases with open fronts, and carefully dusted. He stood on a patterned rug near the freestanding desk in the middle of the room and surveyed the riches with the lift to his heart he always felt in a library.

Behind him, Victory closed the heavy door and muttered some words. At once, the acoustics of the library changed in the distinctive manner of a room protected by a privacy rug.

"Just to be sure," said Victory.

Glancing out of the corner of his eye, he could see an active spell on the runner that was laid around the outer walls.

255

She took him by the arm and drew him towards a reading nook over by the right-hand wall, then guided him to sit on a large couch.

"Now, somewhere over here... Ah!" she said, drawing a book in a plain binding from a nearby shelf and bringing it over. She seated herself next to him, their knees touching, and smiled up at him.

"This is what I wanted you to look at."

He opened the volume and turned to the title page. It was written in Elvish.

A Treatise Concerning the Arts of Love, he read. *For the Instruction of the Inexperienced.*

"Inexperienced?" he queried.

"Well, you are, aren't you?" she said. "I made sure to have enquiries made."

He blushed. "Well, yes," he admitted.

"Don't worry," she said, laying a hand on his arm. "So am I. But I've read the book, and it's most... instructional."

He turned a couple of pages and found a diagram. "Hmm, yes, isn't it? Any particular parts I should concentrate on?"

"Yes, these ones, and this one here," she said, pointing to the diagram.

"I *mean* parts of the *book*," he said, laughing, and blushing even harder.

"Oh. Well, I have arranged for a buffet lunch to be served at midday," she said. "I believe we should be able to reach at least Chapter Five by then. This couch is most commodious." She bounced on it a little, and smiled a wicked smile.

"Since you have read the book already," he said, setting it aside and taking her in his arms, "why don't you summarize it for me?"

"How about I read it to you?" she said, standing quickly and stooping to snatch it from the arm of the couch. "I may need to translate a few of the more... technical terms, though most of them are evident from context."

"Why is it in Elvish, anyway? It's not by an elf, is it?"

"Oh, no, it's not nearly that old, and I don't think a book on this subject by an elf would be useful to us. It's to keep servants and young people from reading it, I assume. Though they could learn quite a lot just from the diagrams." She turned a couple of pages. "I will omit the introduction, the author merely justifies his project, and since we have already committed ourselves to his guidance... Chapter 1. Of kissing, caressing, and the variations thereof." She seated herself sideways on his lap and began to read aloud.

When they emerged for lunch, much tousled, Determined declared that of all the many libraries he had visited, this one was definitely his favorite.

The End

Acknowledgements

A good book isn't written alone. My thanks to everyone who helped, especially the following:

My beta readers, Andy Brokaw, Lisa (L.J.) Cohen (watch for her YA SF novel *Derelict*, it's excellent), Gregory Lynn, Ben Rovik of the wonderful Petronaut dieselpunk stories, and Jolene Stone. It's not their fault that I didn't listen to all their suggestions.

My skilled and knowledgeable developmental editor, Kathleen Dale. Her suggestions deepened and strengthened the story and characters, and helped the setting come through more clearly.

My cover designer, Chris Howard. I wanted a cover that's as good as you'd see from a major publisher, but which no major publisher would ever commission, and Chris delivered. Thanks again to Lisa Cohen, because when I saw Chris's cover for her book I knew I had to have one.

My wife, who puts up with my writing. My employers, who let me work a nine-day fortnight so that I can have time to write. John Ward and all the other Google+ folks, who talk writing intelligently.

And, of course, you. Without readers, the book is just self-indulgence.

Thank you for reading our novel, **Realmgolds: The Gryphon Clerks (Book 1)** and for supporting speculative fiction in the written form. Please consider leaving a reader review so that other people can make an informed reading decision.

Find more great stories, novels, collections, and anthologies on our website.
Visit us at DigitalFictionPub.com

Join the Digital Fiction Pub newsletter for **infrequent** updates, new release discounts, and more:
Subscribe at - Digital Fiction Pub

See just some of our exciting fantasy, horror, crime, and science fiction books on the next page.

More Gryphon Clerks

Realmgolds is part of a series of books in the same setting.

Beastheads goes more deeply into the diplomatic mission to the beasthead lands and the mismanaged attack from Turfrae.

Hope and the Clever Man tells the story of the team that invented the farviewers and farspeakers, and expands on the events that led to Gnome Day. *Hope and the Patient Man* continues their story.

Each book is written to be self-contained, but also refers to characters and events in other books in the series. *Realmgolds*, *Beastheads* and *Hope and the Clever Man* also overlap in time.

You can get the other books in the series from Amazon:

Beastheads
Hope and the Clever Man
Hope and the Patient Man

To find out more, to sign up for notifications of new books coming out, and to get free access to a 40,000-word collection of short fiction in the Gryphon Clerks setting, go to: http://csidemedia.com/gryphonclerks/membership

About the Author

Mike Reeves-McMillan lives in Auckland, New Zealand, surrounded by trees.

He's almost certainly the world's only steampunk-fantasy author who holds a master's degree in English, a certificate in health science, an Advanced Diploma of Hypnotherapy *and* a certificate in celebrant studies (rituals for transition through crisis). He's worked as an editor for a major publishing house, which is just one of the reasons he has no interest in being published by a major publishing house.

He blogs at http://csidemedia.com/gryphonclerks.

Copyright

Realmgolds: The Gryphon Clerks (Book 1)
Written by Mike Reeves-McMillan
Cover illustration by Chris Howard (saltwaterwitch.com)

This story is a work of fiction. All of the characters, organizations, and events portrayed in the story are either the product of the author's imagination, fictitious, or used fictitiously. Any resemblance to actual persons or bureaucrats, living or dead, would be coincidental and quite remarkable.

Realmgolds: The Gryphon Clerks. Copyright © 2017 by Digital Fiction Publishing Corp. and Mike Reeves-McMillan. This story and all characters, settings, and other unique features or content are copyright Mike Reeves-McMillan. Published under license by Digital Fiction Publishing Corp. Cover Image designed and created by Chris Howard and Copyright © 2017 Mike Reeves-McMillan. This version first published in print and electronically: January 2017 by Digital Fiction Publishing Corp., LaSalle, Ontario, Canada. Digital Science Fiction and its logo, and Digital Fiction Publishing Corp and its logo, are Trademarks of Digital Fiction Publishing Corp.

All rights reserved, including but not limited to the right to reproduce this book in any form, electronic or otherwise. The scanning, uploading, archiving, or distribution of this book via the Internet or any other means without the express written permission of the Publisher is illegal and punishable by law. This book may not be copied and re-sold or copied and given away to other people. If you're reading this book and did not purchase it, or it was not purchased for your use, then please purchase your own copy. Purchase only authorized electronic or print editions and do not participate in the piracy of copyrighted materials. Please support and respect the author's rights.

DIGITAL FICTION
PUBLISHING CORP

DigitalFictionPub.com

Made in the USA
Charleston, SC
23 January 2017